CREOLE CURSE

An assignment that sends Jason Brand to New Orleans quickly turns into a nightmarish hunt for three missing young women and an investigation of the death of another. Brand finds himself swimming in a mix of murder and betrayal, with a dash of voodoo thrown in. Then he uncovers the fact that a group of prominent businessmen have also gone missing. After he is almost thrown into the bayou to become food for the alligators, he decides it's time to fight back . . .

NEIL HUNTER

◆

CREOLE CURSE

Complete and Unabridged

LINFORD
Leicester

First published in Great Britain in 2016

First Linford Edition
published 2018

A catalogue record for this book is available
from the British Library.

ISBN 978–1–4448–3558–8

Published by
F. A. Thorpe (Publishing)
Anstey, Leicestershire

Set by Words & Graphics Ltd.
Anstey, Leicestershire
Printed and bound in Great Britain by
T. J. International Ltd., Padstow, Cornwall

This book is printed on acid-free paper

La Nouvelle-Orléans, Louisiana

Netta Delacort, twenty years old, a young pretty woman, when she had been alive, was found dead, her body severely mutilated, in a New Orleans back alley. She was the daughter of Oliver Delacort, a wealthy and well-connected man, who had reported her missing to the local law two weeks earlier. The local police, who already had two other missing girls on their hands, were baffled. Delacort, sensing the problems the local law was having, asked for help through his connections in Washington. He had been a big contributor to the election funds that had gone towards President Grover Cleveland's success in being voted into office, and Delacort made his plea to the very man he had helped.

The President, aware of the strong support he had gained from Delacort and like-minded people, acted on the request and passed it to the man he had recently had dealings with on other matters. He had quickly come to understand the excellent work done by Frank McCord's covert Justice Department operation, and he called McCord to his office, laid out the details of the problem and asked for McCord's help.

'This is a delicate situation. The victims have all come from influential families. The local law appears to be at a standstill. I believe a fresh perspective is called for here. Someone from out of town as it were . . .'

McCord understood the President's predicament. The man was still making his mark. He wanted to show his support for the people who had boosted his chances of getting into office and do something positive.

'I can send a man down to New Orleans, Mr. President. He can look into this and offer assistance to the local law. As you say, fresh eyes on the scene might help. Leave it with me, sir.'

When McCord walked out of the Presidential Office, he had already made up his mind who he was going to send. Maybe not the most diplomatic of his men, but one who would turn over every stone in Crescent City in order to find out what was going on. If there was a way of digging out a crazed killer it needed a man with an edge to do it.

And Jason Brand needed the challenge. Since his return from the assignment in San Francisco, his clash with the Tong, and his partnering with Bodie, Brand had been restless. He had spent time with Victoria Maitland and his son, Adam, but now he was starting to exhibit those caged lion tendencies McCord recognized well.

* * *

'I received the telegram saying you were coming,' Inspector Noonan said.

Brand shook the man's hand, aware

3

of the strength there. Donald Noonan, late thirties, was a solid, handsome man, his light hair just showing gray around the edges. The mustache on his upper lip was neatly trimmed. He regarded Brand with a frankness that could have been intimidating if he had been the kind to take offence.

'So you're from the Justice Department? The telegram didn't go into much detail about you, or your department.'

Noonan waved Brand into one of the chairs in front of his desk. His office was neat. Functional. Books on criminal law in a case against one wall. Louisiana flag in one corner. A few photo images arranged in tidy rows.

'We don't tend to make ourselves known in general.'

'Sounds interesting, Mr. Brand.'

'Times are it can be.'

'The telegram hinted you have instructions to . . . '

Brand held up a hand. 'Inspector Noonan, I'll make myself clear. Last

4

thing I intend is to override your authority here. This is your town and I'm a guest. You don't need some stranger walking in and taking over your investigation. My job is to help in any way I can. I get my orders from Washington and this time they said go to New Orleans and help. My boss got his orders from a higher authority and handed them to me. So here I am.'

Noonan nodded thoughtfully, leaned back in his seat.

'You want coffee?'

'That would go down nicely.'

When they had mugs of strong, hot coffee Noonan took a sheaf of papers from his desk drawer and handed it across.

'Everything we have on the victims. The missing ones and the murdered girl. Backgrounds. As much of their movements before they vanished. And the medical report on Netta Delacort.'

'This one makes three,' Brand commented. 'I'd wager you're getting some aggravation from the families?'

'From all sides,' Noonan said. 'From the victims' families and from my superiors. Now I expect it from the families but not my own people. We're doing our best with what little we have. It's never enough. They expect miracles and when I can't produce . . . ' Noonan buried his head in his mug and took a long swallow. 'I'm no fool. No one in the station wants to get involved because they're all worried about being held to account. So they stay out of sight and allow me to take all the blame. That sounds like I'm whining about how hard my job is. I'm not. Just saying *how* it is. Doesn't inspire confidence and people in certain quarters are not slow in pointing that out.'

'It sounds like you've been chosen as the whipping-boy,' Brand said.

'The higher you get on the promotion ladder the riskier your position becomes. So the best option is to make those under you take the punches. Mr. Brand, I have a good squad of officers with me. We are doing our best here.'

'You'll get no criticism from me. And the name's Jason. Easier than adding titles.'

'Then it's Donald. That comes from my family way back. Scotland. But I prefer Don.'

Brand spent a while going over the written reports, noting a number of points.

'The dead girl was left in an isolated spot. After dark and not found until the next day. She showed marks on wrists and ankles that suggested she had been tied for some time before her death.'

'If you feel it might be helpful we could go and talk to the doctor who carried out the post mortem.'

'That might be a good idea. Few questions I need to ask.'

'We can go now if you want.'

They were preparing to leave when the office door swung wide and a tall, expensively dressed man entered the office. He hadn't knocked to announce himself. Simply swept in and fixed

Inspector Noonan with a sour expression on his lean face.

'I see you are doing nothing again, Noonan, except sitting around drinking coffee with one of your . . . '

'*Monsieur* Lacroix, as you are so fond of telling me, where are *your* manners? Is this the way to impress a guest?'

Lacroix rounded on Brand, who had remained in his seat. He looked at him with a haughty expression on his thin-featured face.

'Who is this man?'

'Ask me politely and maybe I'll tell you.'

'How dare you address me so?'

The voice was cultured, tinged with a degree of superiority.

'Touchy, isn't he,' Brand said.

'I am Victor Lacroix. You plainly have no knowledge of who I am.'

Brand stood, a good few inches taller than the lean man he faced.

'Jason Brand. I hope the rest of New Orleans comes across as a damn sight

8

politer than you, friend. And, no, I don't know who you are.' He glanced at Noonan. 'Should I be worried?'

'Only if you feel inclined.'

'Then there's nothing more to say,' Brand said. He stared down Lacroix until the man retreated a step.

'When you have acquainted yourself with New Orleans, sir, you will understand my position.'

'*Inspector* Noonan and I were about to start our investigation into the death of Miss Delacort, so if you'll step aside we can move out.'

Lacroix's face flushed. 'I want to know anything you learn. *It is . . .* '

'Is this feller an officer of the law?' Brand asked.

Noonan, holding back a smile, shook his head.

'Then I suggest you don't interfere with this investigation,' Brand said. 'Stay out of the way, *mister*. Especially my way.'

'I demand to be kept informed about your progress.'

'Demand all you want, feller. They have newspapers in this town?' Brand asked Noonan.

'Oh, yes,' Noonan said.

'There you go then,' Brand said. 'You can read about it in the next edition.'

'Your attitude could bring you a lot of trouble.'

'Now you've got my attention. I don't like to be threatened. Especially by self-important upstarts like you, Lacroix. I'm trying to figure just what your interest is in all this. When I do maybe we can have another conversation. For now I suggest you leave. Same way you came in.'

'I am here because of concern over a dead young woman and two other missing girls. As an important member of New Orleans society I am of course interested.'

'Well I'm impressed all to hell,' Brand said.

Lacroix turned to leave, pausing to speak.

'You have made a mistake, sir. Be

careful it does not come back at you.'

He strode out of the office, leaving Brand considering what had been said.

'That's me put in my place.'

'That man is a damned nuisance,' Noonan said.

'He as important as he makes out?'

'Lacroix has an image of himself as that.'

He took a pistol from his desk and eased it into the belt holster under his coat. He picked up his hat and gestured for Brand to follow him out.

'What's his story?' Brand asked.

'Victor Lacroix. Extremely wealthy. Old New Orleans money from a family of long standing, although there is only himself and his sister, Seraphina, left alive. He has a wide circle of equally wealthy friends. They dominate the social circle in the city. Have town houses and estates out of the city. Lacroix has contacts all over. He's on familiar terms with influential people.' As they stepped out of the building,

Noonan stopped, putting a hand on Brand's arm. 'Jason, I enjoyed seeing you stand up to that man, but I'd not feel right if I didn't warn you. He'll not let it go. People do not talk to Victor Lacroix the way you did. Just watch yourself.'

'Grateful for the warning. I'm more concerned about how he got to know who I was so fast. You were only sent a telegram direct to your station.'

The implication was not lost on Noonan and he fell silent as they continued along the street.

*   *   *

Doctor Regis Marcellus was middle-aged, looked younger, and had an outgoing manner that he passed to his visitors. He took them into his crowded, book-lined office, sat them down and stood facing them. He was medium height, thin and sported a fashionable mustache that he kept stroking. The dark suit and white shirt he wore hung loosely on his spare frame.

'Mr. Brand is assisting me on the murdered girl's case and the two that are missing,' Noonan said by way of an introduction. 'He's here on official business from Washington. Justice Department. I would appreciate it if you could bring him up to date on what we have.'

Marcellus managed a wry smile. 'That will not take long,' he said in a slow, pronounced local accent. 'Have you read the report?'

Brand nodded. 'Is there anything more you can add?'

'Not really. The girl was badly treated before she was killed. I should say murdered.'

'There was a mention of sexual mutilation in your report.'

Marcellus sighed. A sad sound that expressed the distress he had over the revelation.

'The girl had been subject to repeated sexual penetration. Very brutal

13

attacks. External bruising suggests multiple rapes.'

'While she was alive — or after?'

Noonan was barely able to prevent himself from gasping at the suggestion.

'No, no,' Marcellus said, 'Mr. Brand's question is quite legitimate. In fairness I can understand his reasoning and to be honest, from what I was able to judge, I would venture the answer would be yes to both possibilities.'

'Thanks, Doc.'

★ ★ ★

Victor Lacroix glanced up as Jake Durant walked into his office.

'Got your message,' he said.

Durant was a big man. Six feet tall, very broad shoulders and a massive chest. His head sat square on his shoulders with barely any neck. There was something unnerving in his thick features. A large nose set over a thin-lipped mouth that had a permanent downturn. He stared at the world through a dark right eye — his left had been damaged years ago, leaving it milky, with a puckered scar in the flesh round it.

'There is a government man working alongside the police, looking into our victim's death.'

Durant absorbed the information slowly. It was the way his mind worked. Lacroix waited. He understood Durant's affliction, brought on by the long-term damage caused by the injury that had resulted in his losing his eye. He was slow, deliberate, yet once he had taken in any information it remained.

'Could this cause us problems, Mr. Lacroix?'

'If we allow it to,' Lacroix said. 'So I want you to deal with it. Just make sure it doesn't come back to us. This may be a little premature but I do not want this man getting in our way. We need to eliminate him before he starts looking too closely. Make him vanish. Shouldn't be too difficult. Plenty of room in the bayou.'

Durant managed a crooked smile. 'He'll have company. Our gators are always hungry.'

It wouldn't be the first time Durant had arranged for problems to be disposed of in the murky waters of the bayous. The lonely stretches of water, inhabited by alligators and snakes were ideal for the disposal of anyone who presented Lacroix with the need to be removed.

Lacroix knew there was no need to say more. As slow as he was Durant would understand his meaning. Lacroix left it at that, satisfied the man would act. He would choose men who had no connection to Lacroix, or himself. They would simply be hired assassins, carrying out a contract for money. It was not the first time Jake Durant had handed out such an undertaking. He had no concerns about the people who got hurt if they stood in his way. It was necessary to maintain order and to retain his position. In business, as in pleasure,

Lacroix maintained the highest standards. He had worked hard to get where he was and had no intentions of allowing anything — or anyone — to change that.

★   ★   ★

The Mardi Gras celebration was close. Already the city was becoming crowded as visitors poured in. It was the highlight of the year for New Orleans. A chance to celebrate and enjoy the spectacle. New Orleans worked hard and when the opportunity arose it played hard. Each year tried to outdo the previous one, with elaborate costumes and floats. The upcoming celebrations would be no different. As far as Jason Brand was concerned, Mardi Gras would only make his job harder. His initial look into the murder of Netta Delacort and the missing girls was proving to be slow coming up with any results. He was working with very little and it was no help there were no witnesses to the girl's death.

At a later time he would realize that the unprovoked attack on him became the catalyst for everything that happened in its aftermath. When it took place Brand was too busy doing his best to stay alive to even consider there might be a connection.

He left the police station and made his way back to his hotel. It was situated in the French Quarter and it was no more than a ten-minute walk through the busy area. As he strolled, enjoying a cigar, Brand picked up on the mix of people and language. New Orleans blended English, with the *patois* that came from French and Creole. It made for an intoxicating babble of tongues. He passed along the veranda'd sidewalks, his eyes taking in the sights, while his brain worked over the facts he had absorbed from his talk with Inspector Noonan and Doctor Marcellus.

Each of the girls, from wealthy

families had little in common except in the manner of their abduction. There had been no communication from the people who had taken them, so it did not look as if money had been the reason. The dead girl showed she had been held forcibly. That was obvious from the bruises on her face and body. Marks on wrists and ankles and it was impossible to deny the fact she had been subjected to sexual indignities.

There was still much Brand didn't understand. It irked him. He didn't enjoy being in the dark. He needed something. Anything. A small opening to give him a way to figure out who — or what — was behind the murder.

He stood on a corner, scanning the crowds moving back and forth and despite the reason he was in New Orleans he didn't fail to be affected by the atmosphere. The noisy ambience was transmitted and touched him. In the distance, almost lost in the crowds, he could hear music. Tinny and not always in tune, but it was there and it was part of the city.

If this was what it was like before the carnival, what would it be like on the day? Brand found it hard to imagine.

He felt the need to have a drink before he put himself fully back into why he was here in the city. A brief moment to clear his mind. He chose the first saloon he passed, easing his way inside and up to the crowded bar. The bartender was lean, black, his head shaved. He wore a red shirt and a white apron.

'What you want?'

'Beer,' Brand told him.

He waited until the heavy glass was placed in front of him, paid, and turned to observe the crowd. The talk was loud. Cigar and cigarette smoke hung in a bluish haze near the discolored ceiling. For a few minutes Brand was able to forget his work, the grim reason that had brought him to New Orleans. It would have been an experience for Virginia and Adam. A chance to look around the old city. Maybe another time. When his assignment was over. Before McCord sent him out on some other risky deal. He thought that because he had never yet worked a case that presented him with peace and harmony. Brand often found himself wondering if it was something in himself that encouraged the violence he seemed to encounter. He didn't dwell on that. It would have been too easy to slip into a melancholy mood. He drank his beer, watched the crowd, and let his thoughts drift.

When he felt the sharp prick of something sharp push through his clothing and into his right side he stopped his mental wandering, came back to reality.

'No dumb moves, friend. This knife is very sharp and I got no religion when it comes to using it.'

The voice came from close. Close enough that Brand could feel breath on his cheek. Hot, spicy breath. As if to emphasize the threat the sharp tip of the knife was pushed in a little harder.

'Listen to what he says,' a second voice broke in from Brand's left. 'One push with that blade and you end up on the floor. Not what we want right now, but make it necessary and Rene *will* stick you.'

Rene said, 'We walk out. No fuss. We go right and keep walking until I say otherwise. Just to make it easier for you to understand, my friend has a pistol in his pocket and like me, he will use it if you do something stupid. *To konprann?*'

Brand understood only too well.

The second man took the empty beer glass and placed it on the bar. Brand and his two companions walked out of the bar, turned as they stepped out, and eased their way along the crowded sidewalk.

He took a moment to assess the pair walking alongside him. Rene was thin, with a boney face, shoulder length dark hair. He wore nondescript clothing and scuffed shoes. His partner, taller, with hunched shoulders and a thick body, was pale-haired and showed a haggard face with the broken veins of a drinker.

Brand considered making some kind of break but dismissed the idea. Rene's knife tip stayed where it was and Brand knew it would be a moment's work to thrust it deep. If it failed to kill him outright he could have ended up with a deep wound. He hadn't discounted the other man's handgun. If he started using that some innocent bystander could get hurt. The same applied to Brand's own weapon. In his current situation he wasn't going to have much of a chance to use it on this crowded street.

'Down here,' Rene said. They stepped into a narrow way between buildings.

Rene's partner produced his pistol and held it on Brand.

'Take a look now,' he said.

Rene made a swift, knowing search, and slipped the adapted Colt from the shoulder holster. He showed it to his partner.

'Hideaway gun,' he said. 'This is a sneaky feller, Lupe.'

Lupe grinned. There were gaps in his discolored teeth.

'He won't sneak around those damn gators.'

'Now let's go,' Rene said.

Under the two guns Brand was ushered along the narrow walk to the far end where a black, closed carriage waited, a single man behind the two-horse team. The moment they were all seated, with Brand facing his captors the carriage lurched into motion. With the side curtains down there was no way Brand could tell where they were going. He sat back and let the situation develop. Right then it was a waiting game. Brand needed to find out who was behind this move — and why.

★ ★ ★

Some while later Rene spoke up.

'Lupe, open the damn curtains. It is too hot in here.'

'What if . . . ?'

'*If he sees where we're going?* Does it matter now? He isn't coming back. Give the man a last chance to see daylight.' A shrill laugh bubbled from his throat. 'You see, we're not all bad.'

Lupe rolled up the leather curtain and fastened it out of the way. He repeated the move on the other side of the carriage. Light filled the interior. Brand saw they were moving away from the city, out into the surrounding countryside. Around them the lush foliage and close packed trees told him they were moving into the Bayou area. He glimpsed water through the trees, gleaming in the slanting shafts of hazy sunlight.

'You better like water,' Lupe said, stumbling over his words.

Brand held his tongue and thought about the one chance he might have at getting himself out of this mess.

Inside his right boot was a sheath sewn into the leather. The sheath held a slim, six-inch knife, the handle tight-bound with thin cord to offer the maximum grip. Brand honed the steel blade razor sharp. He kept the existence of the knife known only to himself and it remained his ultimate backup weapon.

Rene said, 'I keep this fancy trick gun. It's nice.'

Lupe only grunted. He slumped back in the seat.

'You always get to keep the best things.'

'Because I am chief. Smarter than you, Lupe.'

Lupe scowled but said nothing. He stared at Brand, his brow furrowing as he worked something out.

'How do you figure that out,' he said after some time. 'You saying I'm stupid?'

'Is this all because of a damn gun?' Rene chuckled. 'If it is so important I will give you the thing when we finish with this one.'

They travelled for at least another

twenty minutes, into denser wooded terrain, thick with heavy grass and foliage. The hot air held a dampness that almost clung to them. Rene abruptly leaned forward and called out to the driver. He hauled the horses round and pulled to a stop.

'*Out*,' Rene ordered.

The ground underfoot was soft, holding a moistness than came from their proximity to the water. Brand heard soft splashes as they cut through, leaving the carriage behind.

'Hear that,' Rene said, relishing the words. 'That'll be the gators waiting to say hello.'

'Those big fellers goin' to love you,' Lupe said. 'You make them good meal.'

★　★　★

The muzzle prodded Brand forward, through the thick grass in the direction of the water. Rene picked up a fist-sized rock and tossed into the dark water of the bayou behind them. The rock made a splash and almost immediately the disturbed form of a large alligator thrust its scaly head into view, massive jaws snapping. It moved back, the water disturbed by its motion, and the massive body could briefly be seen as it slid by.

'Bayou, she got plenty of gators around, an' they always hungry.' Rene waggled the Colt at Brand. 'Now we got to ask a couple questions,' he said.

'You're going to feed me to the damn alligators and now you want me to be cooperative?'

'You answer an' maybe we shoot you instead,' Lupe said.

'That supposed to make me feel better?'

Lupe sniggered. 'Be damn sight quicker.'

'I gotta ask what you found out about the dead girl,' Rene said.

'It going to make any difference if I said I found nothing.'

'You think we're that dumb?' Rene said.

'I could make up something up to keep you happy,' Brand said. 'Or tell you how stupid you really are.'

Rene's short temper exploded and he swung the gun in his hand at Brand, catching him across the side of the head. The blow stung, had less impact than it could have, but Brand played along and gave a pained grunt, letting himself stumble and fall. As he rolled in the grass, onto his side, he hiked up the leg of his pants, sliding his fingers down inside his boot. He grasped the haft of the knife and slid it from the sheath, pulling his hand close to his body.

'You think you killed him?' Lupe asked. 'You can't until we get what Durant wants to know.'

'*Des clous!*' Rene muttered. 'I didn't hit him that hard. Come on, you faker, get up . . . '

He leaned over and took hold of Brand's coat, turning him over. The blade of the knife caught sunlight as it arced up and around, Brand thrusting it directly into Rene's body, twisting and

29

slicing. Blood began to surge from the ragged gash. Rene gave a strangled gasp, and Lupe, not sure what was happening, stepped to the side to see, his hand bringing his own gun up, muzzle searching for a target.

'Hey, what . . . ?'

Brand had yanked the knife free with his left hand and snatched the pistol from Rene's relaxed grip with his right as the man began to fold over him. He leaned around the man's sagging form, picked up on Lupe's large frame as he extended the gun, snicking the hammer back. The Colt cracked out a hard sound, the .45 slug punching in over Lupe's left eye. Brand was not in the mood to be lenient. He pulled the trigger a second time, placing the slug through the top of Lupe's skull as the big man bent over. Lupe jerked in a violent spasm before his legs gave way and he fell forward onto his face, the back of his head a bloody mess. His finger tightened in reflex and his own pistol blew a gout of flame, the slug thudding into the ground.

Rene was partway to his knees, one hand clamped tightly over the bleeding wound. It pulsed between his fingers. He was cursing wildly, his free hand swinging at Brand in a wild punch. Brand shouldered the slight figure aside, sending Rene stumbled backwards, his feet slipping from the grassy bank into the edge of the bayou, splashing noisily . . .

Behind Rene the mass of the gator rose out of the water, the black, reptilian carcass glistening as it surged forward. Rene must have sensed the danger seconds before the reptile struck. The massive jaws opened wide, rows of teeth showing in the moment before they clamped down on Rene's left arm and shoulder. Brand saw the sheer terror on Rene's face as the gator hauled its prey back into the bayou, water splashing in silvery cascades as it shook the suddenly screaming man, jerking him about as if he was nothing but a bundle of rags.

It was over in seconds. The gator submerging, taking the screaming Rene with it, his voice cut off as he was dragged under, and Brand watched, thinking that was what Rene and Lupe had been planning for him. It was a sobering moment as he realized how close he had come.

Brand stuck the bloody knife blade into the ground to clean it before returning it to the boot-sheath and tugging his pants back in place.

He remembered the carriage driver then, something forcing him to turn, bringing the Colt up. Brand saw the dark shape moving out of the trees. The man carried a short-barreled shotgun, the stock held tight against his right hip. The moment he picked up on Brand he jerked the twin muzzles in his direction. Seeing the movement Brand twisted aside, dropping to one knee, the Colt held two-handed as the shotgun fired. He felt the wind of the passing buckshot. Felt his sleeve being tugged. He knew he only had seconds before the man adjusted his aim and let go the second barrel. He took one of those seconds to aim, hold steady and trigger the .45. He felt the pistol jerk against his palm. He took the hammer back again and fired a follow-up shot. The carriage driver took a step back as both slugs pounded his chest. He pulled on the shotgun's trigger and fired the second charge off to one side. As Brand rose to his feet the man toppled, hitting the ground flat on his back, the shotgun slipping from his hands.

New Orleans was turning out to be less than hospitable.

Brand's assignment was barely started and he had been targeted. He recalled what Rene had said.

'*I gotta ask what you found out about the dead girl.*'

That said it all. Whoever was behind Rene and Lupe knew why Brand was in the city. The reason for his visit to New Orleans.

His presence in Crescent City was no secret, Brand admitted. On the other hand, it was not something that had been widely spoken about. McCord would have telegraphed Inspector Noonan and Brand wouldn't have expected the policeman to have broadcast the imminent arrival of someone from the Justice Department.

So how had the news got out?

For a brief moment Brand thought about Noonan himself. Could the leak have come from the Inspector? It was not beyond the realm of possibility, but Brand, who felt himself a good judge of character dismissed the idea. If he was wrong he would find out sooner or later.

Brand moved on. He thought about the telegraph operator. The man would have picked up the details of Brand's arrival in the city and the reason he was there. Right now that was a single lead. Worth looking into once he returned to the city and spoke to Noonan.

The Colt special, quickly reloaded, was returned to the shoulder holster under his jacket as Brand picked up the Greener the carriage driver had dropped. He searched the dead man's coat and found a number of cartridges. He broke the action, extracted the spent shells and reloaded. He felt a little more secure with the loaded shotgun in his hands.

He located the carriage, climbed aboard and picked up the reins. Turning the carriage he set off through the wooded area and made the return trip to the city.

* * *

'If I *was* involved,' Noonan said, 'of course I wouldn't admit it, and I can understand why you might think it.'

They were seated in Noonan's office.

The police officer had listened to what Brand had to tell him. When Brand had mentioned his initial suspicions Noonan even managed a thin smile.

'Natural enough reasoning. I took the telegraph message so I knew you were coming. It would have been easy for me to have informed my . . . '

'*Accomplices?*'

'Whoever they are.'

'When the message arrived was it brought directly to you?'

'As far as I understand. The telegraph office is one floor down. All the officer had to do was walk up the stairs and hand it to me.' When Brand waited in silence Noonan added, 'George Kenworthy. We have two operators. They work shifts and Kenworthy was on duty when the message from your Mr. McCord came through.'

'Begs the question — how did those men learn about my presence? And why I was here. Those fellers I tangled with knew about the dead girl. Their names — Rene and Lupe — they mean anything?'

Noonan shook his head. 'From what you said they sound like a pair of hired thugs. Plenty of those around New Orleans.'

'What about Durant? Way I heard it

those two were working on his behalf.'

Noonan showed interest then. 'You sure that was the name you heard? *Durant?*'

'More than sure. You know that name?'

'Jake Durant? Yes, I know that name. This will interest you. Durant is in the employ of Victor Lacroix . . . '

'The Lacroix who showed up here in your office?'

'The very same.'

'He shows up soon after I arrive. Then I get involved with that pair Rene and Lupe who know Durant and we're back to Lacroix. Maybe I should be concentrating my efforts on him.'

'He's a bad man to cross.'

'Hell, aren't they all.'

Brand stood and crossed to stare out the window, watching the crowds. The Mardi Gras was attracting many visitors to the city. Brand was fast realizing his investigation was not going to be easy. Lacroix had sway in the city. He was wealthy and had people he could call on. Brand didn't allow that to deter him. If Lacroix was behind the killings and pulling strings to manipulate matters it was going to make for an interesting situation. A challenge. And one thing Jason Brand thrived on was a challenge.

★ ★ ★

Inspector Noonan turned at the tap on his door.

'Come in.'

The uniformed constable, young and lean, stepped inside, closing the door behind him.

'You find him?' Noonan asked, anticipating the answer by the expression on the officer's face.

'No one at the hotel has seen, or heard from Mr. Brand since he left this morning, Inspector. The only piece of information I did learn was he asked directions to a livery so he could hire a horse.'

'We need to . . . '

'I already asked at the stable. I know the man who owns the livery. When I described Mr. Brand, Felcher said he rented him a horse.'

'Thinking like that is liable to get you promoted, Kelso.'

'Brand asked for directions for a location out of the city,' Kelso added.

'Let me guess. Victor Lacroix's estate?'

'How did you know that?'

Noonan smiled. 'By being smart, Kelso. That's how I got *my* promotion.'

Lyle Kelso waited, wondering what the Inspector would decide. Noonan stared out the office window. Brand had made it clear he had his own ideas how to deal with Lacroix following the earlier attempt on his life. Noonan was sure the man was experienced enough to look after himself, yet he also knew Lacroix's reputation. If Brand got too close and threatened Lacroix, the man would protect himself. Brand had yet to come up with solid evidence that the man was involved in the disappearance of three young women and the possible involvement in the death of Netta Delacort. Working at doing just that might easily place Brand in a dangerous position, and despite being experienced he would be facing Lacroix's influence and wealth.

'If there is anything I can do, Inspector . . .'

Noonan glanced at Kelso. The young policeman was so eager to prove himself. Perhaps there was a way he could help.

'Go home,' he said. 'Get out of uniform. I don't want you looking like a law officer. Don't tell anyone in the station what you're up to. Kelso, this is important. No one in the station must know what you're doing. Understand? *No one.*'

'Yes, Inspector.'

'Keep your head over this, Kelso. No heroics. I want you to remain out of sight and keep watch on George Kenworthy. Keep this between the two of us.'

'Is Kenworthy in trouble, Inspector?'

'That's what I want to find out. Kelso, this is important. If what I'm about to do proves correct then I will find out that what I suspect is true. If I'm wrong no harm will have been done. Watch for Kenworthy leaving the station. Follow him and observe. Nothing more for the present, just see where he goes. To be on the safe side, make sure you're armed. A precaution you understand.'

'You can depend on me, Inspector.'

'Remember that this must be kept between ourselves.'

'Anything I should know, Inspector?'

'I especially want to hear if Kenworthy visits *The Creole Queen*. I am hoping my suspicions are confirmed over this. Do you know the place?'

Kelso smiled. 'Let's say I've heard about it. Not somewhere I could go myself, Inspector. Too expensive on my pay. Is this to do with Mr. Lacroix? Wasn't he here earlier?'

Noonan nodded. The young officer

was sharp. Didn't seem to miss a thing.

'I'll let you know later. First follow my orders and we'll take things from there if things work out.'

When Kelso had gone Noonan sat behind his desk and considered his next move where Brand was concerned. The man hadn't given much away on where he was going. Noonan couldn't help wondering how far Brand trusted him now it was obvious there was someone within the police station who was giving out information. And after the incident that had almost led to Brand's death Noonan didn't blame him. The Inspector had to own up to the fact his department had not progressed very far where the case was concerned. That fact alone worried him *and* embarrassed him. Noonan was not upset by the fact Brand had been sent to New Orleans. The only thing that did matter was solving the crimes and preventing further murders.

The name that kept bothering Noonan was Victor Lacroix.

Was he linked to the abductions? To the death of Netta Delacort?

The inescapable fact that Jake Durant was somehow involved hadn't escaped Noonan's thoughts either. The man worked for Lacroix. He had dubious connections with the fringes of the criminal society of New Orleans and Brand had picked up his name from the men who had attacked him.

And whether he liked it or not, Lacroix appeared to have been informed about Brand's presence in the city. Too quickly for Noonan's liking. That fact alone only increased the Inspector's suspicions about an informer somewhere within the ranks of the police. It angered him there was an individual leaking information — it also saddened him that somewhere within the ranks of police officers there was a *traitor*. The word came to his lips unbidden. Noonan wasn't naïve enough to see the world as free of corruption, even within the police force, yet it still hurt as he realized that it existed within his own building.

Noonan knew he had to find the culprit. Expose him and deal with him.

Sometime later with Kelso ready to follow his instructions Noonan put his plan into action. It seemed a simple-enough solution. He just hoped it would work.

Taking a sheet of paper Noonan wrote a brief few sentences down, folded the sheet and slipped it into his pocket. He took his police revolver from the desk and checked it was loaded, tucking it in the holster that rode high on his belt, hidden beneath his coat. He stepped out of his office and made his way downstairs and out of the building. He walked for a while until he reached a bar where he knew he could find one of his informants. The man he was looking for was seated at a table, nursing a beer. When he saw Noonan the man barely acknowledged him. Noonan picked up a beer for himself and carried it across to where the man sat.

Caleb Lamar was a middle-aged Mulatto, his skin tone denoting his mixed-race heritage. He earned his living buying and selling information and Noonan had used him on a number of occasions. Lamar, despite his occupation, was a man of principle as far as he could practice. Noonan respected the man and trusted him.

'What may I do for you today, Inspector?' Lamar asked. He always spoke in a quiet tone, never raising his voice.

'I want you to send a telegram to me,' Noonan said. He smiled at the puzzled expression that crossed Lamar's face. 'I have my reasons but the less you know the better for us all.'

Lamar took a swallow of his beer. 'Not for me to question your motives, Inspector. This is official business I understand?'

Noonan simply inclined his head. He took the folded paper from his pocket and slid it across the table. He also added a twenty-dollar bill.

'Should cover the costs of the telegram and leave some for your trouble.'

Lamar slid the paper and the banknote out of sight.

'How soon do you need me to send the telegram?'

'In about a half hour,' Noonan said. He drank his beer. 'Enough time for me to walk back to the station and sit behind my desk.'

Lamar nodded. 'One day perhaps you will be able to explain the reason for this,' he said.

'One day I will, Caleb. That's a promise.'

Noonan stood and walked away without hurrying and took his slow walk back to the station, retracing his earlier steps. As he crossed the street to enter the building he gave a brief nod to Kelso who was nearby, with his face hidden by a newspaper. Back in his office he shed his coat and sat behind his desk, reading through reports he needed to catch up on. He called for one of the constables to bring him a mug of coffee and placed it on his desk while he continued checking the reports.

Donald Noonan was not given to anxiety but he found himself checking the wood-cased clock on the wall of his office. Almost an hour had passed since his return. He was hoping his subterfuge would bring a positive result. His concern was eased when a tap on his door announced a visitor.

'Come in.'

Noonan kept his expression neutral when his door was opened and a uniformed constable stepped into his office because the man was the one he had been hoping would show up.

George Kenworthy, the telegrapher.

Kenworthy, a balding, lean man in his thirties, wearing steel-rimmed spectacles, held a folded sheet in his hand.

'This came for you, Inspector.'

'Thank you, Kenworthy.'

Noonan took the paper and scanned it. The message was word for word as he had written out for Lamar to dictate.

'Do I need to wait for a reply?' Kenworthy asked.

Noonan displayed a casual demeanor, shaking his head.

'No. This is just something I've been waiting for. All the information I require to advance my investigation. Thank you, Kenworthy.'

'Yes, sir.'

The man turned and left. Noonan waited a moment then stood at the part-closed door and watched the man walk quickly to the top of the stairs that led to the ground floor. Maybe he was mistaken but Noonan was sure Kenworthy looked nervous.

* * *

Noonan kept checking from his office window. He could see Kelso waiting across the street. The young man was remaining at his post. Noonan figured the officer would stay on watch as long as it took. It was almost an hour later when Kelso moved, casually crossing the crowded street and turning away from the station. When Noonan leaned forward to see what had alerted Kelso he caught a glimpse of George Kenworthy. He checked the time and saw it was Kenworthy's lunch break. The man had hurriedly left the building and was making purposely away from it. As Noonan watched, he saw Kelso follow the telegrapher and disappear from sight. Noonan experienced a degree of satisfaction. It seemed his ploy might be working. All he could do now was wait for Kelso to report what Kenworthy was up to.

★ ★ ★

It was not difficult for Kelso to keep Kenworthy in sight. The man took his time, making no efforts to conceal his direct approach to *The Creole Queen*, the establishment owned by the man called Lacroix. Kenworthy walked to the alley beside the building and down it until he came to wooden gates that led to the delivery area. Kelso had paused at the head of the alley so he was able to observe Kenworthy's actions. Once the man had gone in through the gates Kelso made his way to them. He paused, uncertain how to proceed. Inspector Noonan was hoping to gain information of Kenworthy's business and the fact he had come to *The Creole Queen* was proving he was on the right track. Kelso decided he had to follow this through. If Kenworthy was making contact with Lacroix, there had to be an important reason. Kelso touched the revolver under his coat to reassure himself. He eased himself through the gates and made his way across the yard. He was making for the loading ramp and the door that would give him access to the main building. He was nervous. He understood the risk he was taking but his need to prove himself to Inspector Noonan overrode caution.

He stepped up onto the loading bay

and moved to the door. It stood ajar. With his hand on his revolver Kelso eased the door open and went through. The interior was shadowed, the place obviously a storage area.

And George Kenworthy was standing a few feet away, facing Kelso.

'What are you doing here, Kelso? Are you spying on me?'

'Maybe with good reason,' Kelso said.

'Noonan. It was Noonan who sent you.' Kenworthy's face flushed with anger as he realized he had been found out.

A large, dark bulk materialized from the shadows and pushed past Kenworthy. It was Jake Durant, his broad face creased by a brutish grin.

'Sonofabitch copper,' he mouthed. 'Sneaking around where he shouldn't be.'

'If Noonan sent him, he must be figuring things out,' Kenworthy said.

'Is that right, bucko? Durant said.

Kelso grasped his revolver and

started to pull it from under his coat. It was a futile move. Durant, big as he was, closed the gap between them in long strides. His left hand closed over Kelso's, crushing his fingers against the butt of the gun. Before Kelso could react, Durant's massive left fist swept in and slammed against the side of his face, the impact knocking Kelso off his feet. Helpless from the powerful blow Kelso dropped, slamming onto the floor with force enough to scramble his senses. Kelso had the taste of blood in his mouth, pain erupting before everything went black . . .

★　★　★

Brand rode past the gates to Victor Lacroix's large house, standing in its own expansive grounds. He made little show of his passing, but mentally retained what he had seen. Depending on how things turned out he might have to pay a second — discreet visit. One thing did catch his attention. A man seen through the bars of the main gate. He was making no attempt to conceal the shotgun carried in the crook of his arm. Not an unseen sight. Just Lacroix securing the safety of his property.

Maybe.

Or because he had something to hide.

A question that needed an answer.

★ ★ ★

Noonan was starting to get anxious. George Kenworthy had returned to the station but there was no sign of young Kelso. Something was not right. A feeling of guilt edged Noonan's thoughts. Had something happened to Kelso? He had sent the officer to trail Kenworthy and now he seemed to have disappeared. If Kenworthy had returned to the station there was no reason why Kelso should not have come back as well.

So where was he?

The afternoon was coming to an end. Once darkness fell it would be difficult to locate Kelso if Noonan went looking for him.

Noonan glanced at the clock on the wall. Kenworthy's shift would be ending shortly. The Inspector decided it was time he did something useful like following Kenworthy and confronting him.

When Kenworthy left the station, Noonan was waiting. He fell in behind the man and kept him in sight as Kenworthy moved quickly through the busy streets. He realized Kenworthy was not walking in the direction his rooms lay. In fact, he was going in the opposite direction, taking them into a shabbier part of the city.

Was he going to meet someone?

Or leading Noonan into some kind of trap?

The answer revealed itself as Kenworthy scuttled down a trash-littered ally and was waiting when Noonan followed.

'Why are you following me, Inspector Noonan?'

Noonan faced the man, his hand under his coat near his holstered weapon. Even in the fading light Noonan could see a gleam of sweat on Kenworthy's face. He had taken off his spectacles and was wiping the glass with a kerchief from his coat.

'You look nervous, Kenworthy. Why is that? Is it something to do with Officer Kelso?'

'I don't know why it would be about Kelso.'

'Maybe because he followed you earlier and when you came back he didn't.'

'What has that to do with me?' Kenworthy's words came out in a rush. 'He shouldn't have made . . . '

'He was doing his job. On my orders.'

'What right do you have following me? I shall make a complaint, Inspector Noonan.'

'Fine with me, Kenworthy. Let us do that. We'll go back to the station and sit

55

down with the Superintendent and discuss the matter . . . '

Kenworthy made a sound that might have been a protest. At the same time he thrust his hand under his coat and produced a short-barreled revolver. His eyes were wide and staring as he pushed the gun at Noonan and pulled the trigger. Noonan felt a solid thump against the left shoulder, the impact pushing him against the alley's grimy wall. He closed his hand over his own revolver, drawing it with surprising speed and as Kenworthy stepped forward, lining up his weapon for a second shot, Noonan fired, cocked and fired again. The .38 caliber police issue revolver flamed as it sent the two slugs at Kenworthy. They hammered his chest, knocking Kenworthy back and down, his body slumping to the floor of the alley, his pistol bouncing from his hand.

Leaning against the wall Noonan fished out his police whistle and used it to summon help before the pain in his shoulder robbed him of being able to do very much else.

★ ★ ★

By the time Brand arrived back in New Orleans, the shooting between Noonan and George Kenworthy was the talk of the station. Noonan, after being treated by Doc Marcellus, had insisted on returning to speak with his superiors. Brand was directed to the senior officer's office on the top floor, where Noonan sat facing the grim-faced Superintendent, his wounded shoulder bandaged and his arm in a sling.

'I have to say I am disturbed by what has taken place,' the uniformed man said. 'It is a bad day when officers under my command indulge in gun-fights.'

'As I have already reported,' Noonan said, 'my intention was to talk with Kenworthy over a suspicion I had over his behavior. There was no intention to engage in a shooting. I was simply defending myself.'

The Superintendent — a man named Wallace — glanced at Brand.

'It appears you have something of a bad luck streak as well, Mr. Brand. Noonan has apprised me of the attempt on your life. Your appearance in New Orleans seems to have unleashed an epidemic of violence.'

'Seems to me my showing up has rattled someone. When I'm almost offered up as alligator bait I tend to take it personally.'

Wallace sighed, leaning back in his seat.

'I understand how this has become a far-reaching matter. Hiram Delacort has lost his daughter and is naturally distraught. Two other young women have also gone missing and we, as the New Orleans Police Department, have failed to a degree in finding out the perpetrators. I cannot deny that. Delacort asked for higher help and the President deemed it the right way to go. Can't say I'm overly happy with that, but politics aside, the matter concerning those young women is paramount. If bringing an outsider to assist will pacify those involved . . . ' Wallace shrugged, ' . . . then we must abide by the decision.'

'Even if you don't like the idea? I told Inspector Noonan I'm here to help,' Brand said. 'Nothing more. Have to admit Lacroix showing up at Noonan's office the way he did kind of interested me.'

'The man has an inflated image of himself as beyond our reach,' Wallace said. 'His influence in the city makes him feel invulnerable.'

'Perhaps we should let him know that influence doesn't affect us,' Brand said.

'Noonan mentioned Victor Lacroix. Is there a suspicion concerning him?'

'Coming to my office was little more than bravado. And a chance to face Jason because he'd been warned of his coming.'

'Superintendent, he's already slipped up. We've identified Jake Durant as being in his pay,' Brand said. 'And Noonan's faked telegram, naming Lacroix was enough to send Kenworthy running.'

'You've heard nothing more about Officer Kelso?' Wallace asked.

Noonan shook his head. 'I regret sending him. I may have put him in danger. I've assigned as many men as I can to keep an eye out for him.'

'I may have something here that could help,' Wallace said. He picked up papers from his desk. 'It seems the appropriate moment to let you see these. I have been debating what to do but now seems the moment.' He passed the papers to Brand. 'Lacroix has been under suspicion for a while of being involved in illegal activities. We haven't had anything definite to use but now, with current matters, it seems we may have a chance to gain something solid. To be honest, pointing the finger at Lacroix is difficult. He is, shall we say, a slippery customer. And he does have the ear of very influential people.'

'So I keep hearing,' Brand said. 'But *my* influence reaches as high as you can get, so no need to be coy here.'

'The last section came to light a couple of days ago. Henry Dalton, Jerome Cortland and Cyrus Buckman. They all seem to have disappeared.'

Brand waited until Wallace spoke again.

'All three are prominent businessmen in New Orleans. Buckman actually owns a bank. He's extremely wealthy.'

'The connection?'

Wallace cleared his throat.

'They have all been associated with Victor Lacroix. Been seen at his casino, *The Creole Queen*. Eyewitnesses have seen the three regularly sitting in on high stakes poker games. Large amounts of money have been seen on the tables. The three missing men are well known to each other. In their businesses they are all pretty staid, men who abide by the conservative rules of their work.'

'Lacroix runs a pretty lax gambling

house,' Noonan said. 'Patrons can enjoy a drink, smoke expensive cigars and delight in the more dubious pleasures Lacroix has to offer. From what I've heard the girls Lacroix employs are of a high quality. They are led by Lacroix's sister — Seraphina.'

Wallace grunted in disapproval.

'The rumors are that she is a practitioner of the black arts.'

'*Black arts?*'

'Voodoo. A Creole cult,' Noonan said. 'The stories are well told in the area. Voodoo is a strong tradition around New Orleans.'

'Tradition? Real or imagined?'

'Jason, the beliefs are strongly held.'

Brand held back from comment. He knew enough about mystical tradition from his contact with Indian culture. Medicine men. *Shamans*. Strong cultures that were *not* to be passed over lightly.

'It is known that Seraphina Lacroix has a strong influence over her brother,' Noonan said. 'It may simply be talk but

I have heard the pair of them are a whole lot closer than brother and sister ought to be.'

'The more I hear the more I'm convinced I should start with a look at this *Creole Queen*.'

'Before you do,' Noonan said, 'I'd like you to come with me and hear what Eleanor Buckman has to say. She is Buckman's sister.'

★　★　★

In the parlor of Doc Marcellus' home, behind his office Brand was introduced to the sister of Cyrus Buckman. A middle-aged, plump woman who seemed on the edge of panic.

'Mr. Brand, I do not know what has my brother so terrified. I just know it is haunting him. He moans in his sleep as if something terrible is in his dreams. But he refuses to talk about it. If I press him he becomes irritable to the point of . . . and now he appears to have vanished.'

Brand saw the ashen color in her cheeks, the glint of tears in her eyes. Her voice faltered, fading away to barely a whisper. She turned aside, burying her face in her hands. He was glad that Doctor Marcellus's wife was there. She placed her arms around the weeping woman, comforting her with the words Brand could not have spoken. She glanced at him, shaking her head gently.

'Come and sit down, Eleanor. No more talk of these things until you feel ready.'

She guided the trembling woman across the room to a sofa and sat beside her.

'Why do you not take Mr. Brand and the Inspector into the other room,' Katherine said. 'A drink would not be amiss I am sure.'

The other room turned out to be a study, complete with book-lined shelves and comfortable leather armchairs. Marcellus quietly closed the sliding door.

'Whiskey?' he said. Brand nodded. 'Sit down, Jason.'

Noonan shook his head at the offer and favoring his shoulder, took another chair.

Brand took the heavy tumbler and stared at the rich amber liquid. He waited until Marcellus occupied the chair facing his.

'That woman is close to a breakdown,' the doctor said. 'Whatever is ailing her brother is tearing her apart. And now this disappearance.'

Brand tasted the mellow whiskey, his thoughts absorbing him for a moment.

'It's more than simply an affair with a woman,' Noonan said. 'Or gambling debts. It has to be something far worse, and I'm convinced now it has something to do with Lacroix.'

'I'm inclined to agree,' Marcellus said. 'Up until a few months ago Buckman was as steady as any man I've ever known. A solid, respected figure.'

'Doc, I've come across *respected*

fellers I wouldn't trust with a loaded gun.'

'I guess you could be right about that,' Noonan murmured.

Brand said, 'When did those girls begin to vanish?'

Marcellus paused with his glass barely touching his lips. The expression on his face gave Brand the answer before he spoke and even then there was doubt.

'Around three months ago . . . *my God, man*, are you trying to suggest Cyrus Buckman has something to do with them missing?'

'Doc, I'm just trying to get a handle on this mess. Maybe I'm reaching in the dark. Just trying to untangle things. I was hoping Buckman's sister might tell if I'm looking in the right place . . . '

'Have to admit there are questions I'd like answers to myself . . . ' Noonan said.

'I believe Eleanor Buckman might be able to provide some of those,' a voice said. None of them had heard the door slide open to admit Marcellus's wife. 'She wants to see you now.'

Marcellus and Noonan followed Brand back into the parlor where Eleanor Buckman was waiting. Her face was still pale, eyes moist, but she had composed herself enough to face them.

'I must apologize for my behavior,' she said.

'Ma'am, there's no need,' Brand said. He took a seat facing her.

'I cannot in all truth deny my concerns over my brother. His sleep has been disturbed most every night. I've heard him moaning in his room. Walking about. Back and forth. Even awake he seems distracted, as if matters on his mind are disturbing him. His manner is abrupt. Reaching extremes at times. He has never exhibited such extreme behavior before. Now he has gone.'

'Do you have any thoughts why? I understand he has business interests in the city. Could his problems be associated with them?'

'As far as I am aware his business affairs are sound. The bank is successful. Whatever his problems I do not see the bank as being behind them. I believe they . . . ' Eleanor Buckman hesitated, struggling to find the words she needed to express herself, ' . . . are associated with *The Quorum*.'

Brand glanced at Marcellus. He shook his head.

'*Ma'am?*'

'It is the name for a group of his business associates. A small gathering who can step away from the daily pressures of work. A social gathering away from boardrooms where they can relax and enjoy the company of like-minded men. A way of relieving the day to day pressures of business.'

'Yet you say your brother has been far from relaxed?'

'When he first began his association with these men everything seemed fine. He came home from his meetings refreshed and in good humor. Then about three months ago he began to change. The distractions started. The depression and the interrupted sleep.'

Brand caught Marcellus staring at him.

Three months.

The number had come up again.

Three months *since the disappearances began.*

The same time Buckman had started to exhibit changes.

'Do you have names for these men your husband associates with?'

Eleanor Buckman nodded.

'Two of them yes. Jerome Coleman and Henry Dalton. They have been his close friends for many years. Very good friends.'

'Where do they meet? The same place each time?'

The woman nodded. 'At *The Creole Queen.* Victor Lacroix owns the place. My husband and his friends enjoy playing cards there,' Eleanor said, obviously not entirely comfortable. 'And I am sure there are other attractions. I believe you can imagine what I am referring to.'

Brand was sure she was hinting at women.

Marcellus explained. 'Gambling. Entertainment. *The Creole Queen* has a reputation as the place where anything can be had — for a price.'

And Victor Lacroix owned it.

Brand didn't express any surprise at the name. Because he was *not* surprised. Although he had not said anything about his suspicions, Eleanor Buckman's revelation had confirmed what he had been thinking, albeit subconsciously. That Lacroix had a hand in what was happening.

It was starting to add up. Things coming together. There were still loose ends, but a picture was forming through the shadows.

And Victor Lacroix was in there.

So was his sister — Seraphina.

Brand was more than convinced they were both at the back of the affair. As much as he didn't like the thought he was beginning to believe they were responsible for the disappearances and the death of Netta Delacort. He decided he would keep that to himself for the moment. Until he had solid proof. He might be certain in his own mind. Convincing others might not be as easy.

'Will you find Cyrus?' Eleanor Buckman asked.

'I'm going to try,' Brand said.

Noonan said, 'Keep your wits about you, Jason. The Mardi Gras celebrations started today, so New Orleans is going to be crowded more than usual . . . and noisier.'

* * *

Noonan had not been wrong. The streets teemed with a mass of people, many in colorful and garish costumes. Floats trundled and swayed as they negotiated the streets. Music struggled to be heard above the constant racket of voices. Brand found himself seemingly moving against the flow as he made his way to *The Creole Queen*.

The outside was gaudy and bright, windows gilded and adorned with the name of the casino. Observing it from the opposite side of Bourbon Street, Brand had to admit it stood out. He could hear the constant ripple of voices coming from inside, almost drowning out the music playing. If he hadn't been on assignment he could have enjoyed the atmosphere himself, but he had to push that to the back of his mind and concentrate on his duty.

He wore his black suit, his string tie neat against the white shirt. The Colt special rested in the shoulder holster, beneath his coat. Brand entered the casino merging with the crowd who pushed in through the open doors. A drift of tobacco smoke hung overhead, mingling with sweat and liquor. His eyes scanned the brightly lit expanse, taking in the long bar with gleaming mirrors fixed to the walls behind it. Lines of bottles and glasses filled the shelves below the mirrors. Against one wall were long tables showcasing an open buffet where the patrons were able to partake of the free food. A number of aproned waiters slid in and out of the gathering, expertly balancing small drinks trays on their hands. As one moved by him Brand caught a champagne glass and tasted the pale liquid. It was quality and chilled. Lacroix maintained a high standard for his customers. He picked out a number of young, attractive women circulating the room. They stopped and spoke to customers, smiling and laughing at jokes. All part of the business.

Looking beyond the crowd and the gaming tables he saw a door on the far wall that was being watched over by a pair of hard-faced men. Silent and unmovable they could not have advertised their presence more if they showed the revolvers sitting under their coats. As Brand observed he watched as two men approached, spoke quietly to the guards. Both were middle-aged, impeccably dressed and exuded wealth. One of the guards opened the door and let the pair through, then returned to his silent vigil.

Brand was instantly intrigued. Something told him he would be more than interested to see what lay behind that guarded door. He drained his champagne and placed the empty glass on a table as he passed, moving casually in the direction of the door. As he closed in on the door he saw the guards physically tense. His earlier appraisal had told him they were well muscled and placed at the door to deter any unwanted visitors. He stopped within a few feet, a casual smile on his face.

'Going to let me in?'

'Not for you, sir,' one of them said.

'Hey, I'm here to enjoy myself and I have the money to prove it.'

A large hand was raised and held in Brand's face.

The guard's impassive stare was intended to make people back away. It failed to impress Brand. He might have done something rash if he hadn't picked up on someone close behind him.

Turning he came face to face with a slim, groomed figure regarding him with a disarming smile on his face. Stylish clothes, including a ruffled shirt. When the man spoke it was with a cultured French accent.

'I am Julienne Dubois, the house manager. I must inform you that the games are private beyond this door, *Monsieur*. Without an introduction, there's no way of getting in. A member must vouch for you. Strict rules of the house you must understand.'

'Well we wouldn't want to break the rules, *Monsieur Dubois*.'

'That would never do.' Dubois offered a slight bow. 'Your visit to *The Creole Queen* is known and I doubt it has to do with gambling. I will tell you only once *Monsieur* Brand. Do not continue with this. Persist . . . *qui sait*.'

All extremely polite, Brand thought. But he hadn't failed to notice the shoulder-holstered handgun concealed beneath the well-cut coat. Or the cold expression in the Frenchman's eyes. Beneath the elegant *façade* Dubois was as much a killer as any back-alley thug. Not the sort of man he would be advised to offer his back to.

New Orleans it seemed had teeth, sharp and hungry, behind every welcoming smile. It was time Brand started playing hard himself, because if he failed to stay on his toes the local bayou's gators might still get to meet him.

'Another time perhaps,' Brand said and walked away.

He crossed to the bar and ordered a drink. He paid, picked up the glass and turned with his back to the bar so he was able to scan the room. Scattered among the paying customers he picked out more of the establishment's watchers. He counted up three of them. Well-dressed and sharp. All armed under their coats. Not one of them held a drink. Or engaged in any conversation with the customers. Lacroix had his people well trained. The men stood close to the walls. Spaced apart so they could cover the whole room. They were watching. Waiting. The moment anything started they would move in quickly and deal with the situation. Brand had to give Lacroix credit for his organizational skills, yet the more he thought about it the stronger his conviction that Lacroix had more going on than a simple gambling and drinking setup.

Brand had seen enough to know he was getting close to the real reason why Lacroix was so needful of such a strong security force.

He wasn't fully certain what just yet, but he was going to find out.

Gambling and liquor and women were a front to the man's *real* business. *Whatever that was*.

He was convinced there was something he needed to see on the other side of that well-guarded door. Brand emptied his glass, moved casually towards the door and stepped outside. He made his way along to the corner, took a right turn and followed the span of the casino until he reached the alley that ran along what would be the building's side and rear wall. Checking it out he saw a six-foot solid fence with double-gates. That would lead to the delivery yard and storage area.

And even a back exit from the casino.

The gates yielded at his touch and Brand eased through, stepping into the rear yard of the casino. It was only later he realized he should have been suspicious of being able to get inside the yard. By then it was too late.

As he slipped through the gate he reached under his coat and drew the Colt from his belt. The feel of the heavy pistol in his hand gave him a degree of comfort.

Across the hard-packed dirt of the yard he saw the casino's rear wall. A wooden delivery platform and a wide door. To his left he saw a couple of expensive buggies and a small livery stable where he could see the restless shape of horses. Brand moved to cross the yard, heading for the rear door.

He never reached it.

The door opened and an armed figure appeared.

It was Julienne Dubois. The gun Brand had spotted concealed by the man's coat was in Dubois' hand now, the muzzle casually aimed in Brand's direction. It was a Colt Derringer.

As the Frenchman stepped onto the loading platform, two more men showed themselves. They were the pair Brand had confronted in the casino. Still large and threatening — with the addition of their hands resting on the butts of pistols in holsters on their belts.

Brand accepted his mistake and also that he had walked into the trap Julienne Dubois had plainly set for him.

'I did warn you,' Dubois said. 'Offered you the chance to walk away, *Monsieur* Brand.'

'Always had problems with being *told* to do things. In English . . . or French.'

'Your persistence may be your downfall,' Dubois said.

He turned his head slightly to speak to the pair behind him.

Brand had only taken a couple of steps inside the gate while he had assessed the area. Three, four feet at most, the gate still open behind him. As Dubois turned Brand made his move. He had no idea how good a shot the Frenchman was. He was about to find about as he triggered a wild shot at the grouped figures, at the same time turning on his heels and ducking low as he went through the gap in the gates.

He picked up a shout. Followed by a shot. The slug hammered into the edge of one of the gates and Brand felt wood splinters tug at his sleeve. Then he was through, turning down the alley away from the street side.

He had no idea where the alley would lead him, but as long as it took him away from Dubois that was fine. For the moment he had no choice. Staying alive was his paramount objective.

The alley began to curve around to the right. He had no choice but to follow it.

Shots came from behind him, slugs chipping at the alley side. Brand felt one slice his coat sleeve. He kept moving, resisting the urge to turn and fire back. He picked up on raised voices as Dubois urged his people in pursuit.

Brand skidded around the alley bend, one shoulder catching the stone of a wall. The impact made him twist and over his shoulder he saw fast moving figures coming in his direction. Four of them, moving swiftly ahead of Dubois and his slower moving gunmen.

They were dressed in carnival costumes, wearing masks, and wielding machetes. One of them, lean and fast, had drawn ahead of his companions and was coming straight at Brand.

As he pushed away from the wall, almost going to his knees, Brand caught a fleeting glimpse of a grinning face rushing at him. Only it wasn't a natural expression. It was a painted face. Stark white with a black-lipped mouth and wide, black-circled eyes, teeth gleaming. The face had the appearance of a living skull. The figure was dressed all in black, even the hands covered by thin black gloves. The machete clutched in one hand, raised as the man closed in. He made a wild swing that Brand barely ducked away from. As the club skimmed his head he ducked, driving his left shoulder into his attacker's chest. The man let out a choked gasp of breath as Brand kept pushing, driving him back until the side of the closest building brought them up short. Despite his awkward position the man swung the machete down and slammed it flat across Brand's back. There was little power in the strike but it still hurt. Brand pushed his upturned palm in under the exposed jaw, pushing hard and slamming the man's head back. It rapped against the stone wall, the man's teeth snapping shut and biting into his protruding tongue. Blood washed from his mouth in a crimson flood. Brand ignored the warm slickness as it dribbled over his hand. He was concentrating on slamming the man's head against the wall again, putting in as much force as he could. A free hand reached up and gripped Brand's hair, pulling his own head back. Brand felt the tendons in his neck being stretched. With a quick move, he jabbed a stiff finger into one of his opponent's eyes, pushing it in deep and felt the spurt of fluid as he inflicted damage. The man screamed and his resistance slackened, giving Brand the chance to step back and lift the Colt. He didn't hesitate, snapping the hammer back and pushing the muzzle into the soft flesh under the man's jaw and pulled the trigger. The .45 slug emerged from the white painted skull, misting the air with red.

From behind the collapsing figure Brand heard a rising wail of yells and saw a trio of garishly dressed figures rushing along the alley, brandishing more gleaming machetes.

He leveled the Colt, taking swift aim

and firing. His slugs were deliberately placed and punched into exposed legs. Two of the advancing men tumbled, clutching at their wounded limbs. The third man stumbled but came on, raising his machete, eyes wide and staring under the influence of something that had driven him forward. He would have kept coming if Brand had not calmly steadied his gun and put his last shot into the sweat-gleaming forehead. Momentum carried the figure on until his limbs collapsed and he pitched face down on the ground, the back of his head a ruined and bloody mess.

Brand turned away, keeping moving as he ejected the empty casings from his pistol, pulled fresh shells from his pocket and reloaded. As he reached the end of the alley he paused, looking left and right, and admitted he had no idea where he was. He stood with his shoulders resting against the wall behind him. He could hear the moans coming from the two men he had put down and beyond that the ebb and flow of the Mardi Gras celebrations as the crowds surged forward. He decided, reluctantly, he was going to have to take the main street and merge with the crowds. There seemed little else he could do until he reached . . . he almost said *safety* . . . and a thin smile curled his lips.

Safety seemed to be in short supply in New Orleans. The investigation he had started seemed to be falling apart. The only ally he had, Noonan, was out of action. Brand had no idea who he could trust so for the time being he was going to have to depend on the one person he *could* be sure of.

Himself.

He had been doing that most of his life. From the day when the Comanche had struck his family ranch and left him for dead. He had survived and it had been that way ever since. Brand had learned the lesson early and it had stayed with him, becoming that part of him that kept him going when times were hard — or threatening. Frank McCord had told him the day he recruited Brand he would need to be able to operate on his own. That had proved to be true on more or less every assignment he had been given, and his visit to New Orleans had simply maintained the status quo.

★　★　★

He pushed the handgun out of sight and kept moving along the next alley where he could see the carnival crowd still filling the street. With the celebration well under way, losing himself in the crowd might give him the chance to get clear. He needed to get back to the police station where at least he would have some kind of protection.

Brand had no qualms about making a retreat, dignified or not, if the need arose. Making a stand could be justified if there was a chance of walking away from it. Right now Lacroix had him outnumbered and making a stubborn fight that would lead to his death wasn't going to make any sense at all. So his best bet was to distance himself from his pursuers and make a measured response. If he could take down a few of the opposition that would be enough for him in the short term.

Somewhere behind him he could still pick up the strains of the Mardi Gras, the music rising and falling as he weaved his way through the alleys between the buildings. He caught the occasional glimpse of the cavorting crowds between them. At least his moves had drawn his opponents away from the celebrating crowds, leaving them to their enjoyment. They deserved that at least.

He flattened against the side of a building, taking a few moments to allow his breathing to settle. In truth he could have used a longer break, but he knew that Lacroix's followers were not about to allow him too much of that.

Sweat beaded his face, pulled damply at his clothing. He wanted nothing more than a chance to rest. To settle in some place where he could have time to figure out just what was going on.

It wasn't the first time Brand's assignments had him working solo. Left to his own devices to walk through a case. McCord expected his operatives to be able to deal with any assignment purely on his own intelligence. Without involving others if it was possible and Brand was comfortable enough working that way. There were times when having official, or unofficial, assistance helped.

Brand found himself thinking back to the assistance he had been offered by working with the man called Bodie. The taciturn bounty man had showed up a couple of recent times and walked side by side with Brand on tough cases. After a shaky start on the first assignment Brand had admitted having the manhunter at his side had been more than helpful. On the second team up, on a complicated case in San Francisco, Bodie's partnership had seen them through everything thrown in their paths. Brand could have done with the man's presence and his ready gun right now. Bodie's direct way of dealing with situations would have been a real comfort.

* * *

Brand caught the sudden intake of breath as someone braced themselves. It was enough to alert him to a violent movement. He turned half-around and caught the moving figure. A tall and lean dark shape, teeth gleaming in a mouth held in a wild grimace. Gleaming too was the flashing blade of a wild-swung machete. It cut the air as it swept in at Brand's body, high enough to have severed his head if it had landed. He had no time for thoughts of what could have happened if the blade had landed. He simply let himself drop to a crouch. Felt the blade stir the air as it cut over him. Knowing the attacker might easily reverse his strike and bring the blade back at him Brand let his weight fall on his hands, then kicked out with his right foot, the heel of his boot slamming hard against the attacker's left knee. Brand put all of his weight into the kick, felt it connect. The knee shattered, the limb bending against the natural joint and Brand even heard the soft sound of breaking bone. The attacking man let out a high, agonized scream as he felt his leg tear under the blow. The machete spun out of his hand as he stumbled, dropping to the ground.

On the edge of his vision Brand saw a second man moving in. He had halted briefly when he saw his partner go down, screaming in agony, and it was that hesitation that gave Brand the chance to react. He thrust his arm forward, cocking the Colt, and without pause put two .45 caliber slugs in the man. They were both on target, thudding into the man's chest and putting him down without a sound. Swinging the Colt around Brand targeted the first man and sent a slug that slammed into the man's head over his left eye. The force of the slug kicked the man onto his back, a thin mist of blood fanning out the back of his skull.

In the background Brand could hear the raucous, pulsing beat of the Mardi Gras celebrations. Rising and falling, the sound rolled out over the streets, reaching him even as he rose to his full height, the Colt searching the shadows for any more of Lacroix's brethren. Instinct told him they would be close by, still looking.

Hungry for blood.

His blood.

Brand began to move in the direction of the music. Maybe he could lose himself in the crowds of revelers. In the mass of people. He took the moment to shuck out the empty shell casings, thumbing fresh ones from the belt loops. He felt a little better having a full load. Six .45 caliber loads — safety in numbers — he decided.

Even then he was thinking about the dead and the missing. It was what his mission was about. Not him, but about the cruel death of Netta Delacort and the missing young women — and now three men.

Brand dodged into a narrow alley that took him closer to the rising sound, shadow enveloping him until he cleared the far end and stepped out onto the crowded, brightly illuminated main thoroughfare. He slid the pistol behind his belt, drawing his coat over it as he merged with the noisy revelers, feeling himself being pushed along by the exuberance of the crowd.

He was surrounded by men and women, in their gaudy costumes, by moving floats of grotesque figures. He heard music close and far, heard the crackle of firecrackers and smelled the smoke as they burned. The noise swelled and swept over him. Brand let himself be pushed along, caught in the moving stream of humanity. Jostled, almost herded, he went with the flow, the raised voices and the pulse of music all combining to make it hard to stay on top of the threat he knew was still around.

Lacroix's people would still be in the area, mingling with the Mardi Gras masses, working their way forward as they searched for him. There would be men on the fringe of the procession, looking to spot him if he broke free from the main crowd. Whichever way he moved they would be watching for him, searching. Just waiting for the moment when he tried to get himself clear. Brand tried to outguess them. To figure ahead as to what they were going to do.

If one of them could get close enough it would be easy to use a knife. In the crush of bodies it would be a simple strike. A swift thrust and it would be over. Considering the mood Lacroix's men were in, they were not going to be too concerned if anyone else got in the way. Brand understood he was dealing with men too ready to kill. Their own safety would not be a consideration.

He scanned the surging crowd around him. The excited, smiling faces. Costumes. The bobbing and weaving floats. The constant pulse of music. Brand was surrounded by a kaleidoscope of color and noise, the atmosphere almost intoxicating. In a different place and time he could have enjoyed the spectacle. Right now all the Mardi Gras provided was moving cover as he tried to distance himself from Lacroix's people.

He barely heard the shot but felt the wind of its passing. It was only luck that prevented the slug from hitting anyone else, and Brand knew he could not stay with the crowd any longer. Putting others in danger was something he had no right to do. He plunged to the side, pushing his way through the noisy throng.

He stepped into an alley, hearing shouts above the pulsating noise, and knew his pursuers were not giving up. Brand kept moving, his intention to lead them away from the Mardi Gras crowd. As he moved along the alley he saw figures at the far end as he was hemmed in.

There was no place to go. There was a sudden rush of figures, some wielding machetes, others armed with guns. They blocked the alley, converging on Brand's position and despite being armed himself he knew he didn't stand a chance against so many. He backed against the wall, hands out from his sides.

When a burly figure stepped forward, a harsh grin on his scarred face, Brand knew he was facing the man named Durant. The one who had sent the men who had tried to dump him in the bayou as alligator food. He held a large revolver aimed at Brand.

'Coming to New Orleans was your first mistake,' Durant said. 'Second was killing my friends. I'll wager right now you'll be wondering if there's a third coming up.'

'I'm figuring you're about to tell me.'

Durant chuckled.

'Better than that — I'm going to show you.'

* * *

Brand was relieved of his weapon and surrounded by Durant's crew was escorted back to the rear of *The Creole Queen*. As they crossed Bourbon Street Brand noticed that the casino was being emptied. Customers were being escorted out through the front entrance. This time there was no problem getting inside. He was taken in through the gates, then through the door on the loading platform and through the storage area. The door they then entered led into what Brand saw a well-appointed room, with card tables and comfortable, upholstered chairs. A door on the far side would be the one that Brand had been hoping to get through earlier. He was in the room now but he couldn't see it was going to do him any good.

There were four people in the room.

A young fellow who looked as if he had undergone a hard beating. He was slumped against the wall, half-conscious. Brand took a guess this would be Lyle Kelso, Noonan's missing officer.

He recognized the smirking face of Julienne Dubois. The Frenchman was watching Brand with a look of *I told you so* on his face.

And there was a young woman, reclining in one of the upholstered chairs, idly toying with a stack of ivory poker chips. Brand saw immediately she was beautiful. Dark-haired and with, even sitting down, a lithe and shapely body. When she glanced up, fixing her steady gaze on him Brand saw the likeness to Victor Lacroix. This had to be the sister.

Seraphina Lacroix.

A gentle upturn of her full lips suggested she found the situation amusing.

Beautiful, yes, he had to accept, but there was a look in those dark eyes that told him of inner coldness. She would not be a woman to trust. Not in the slightest.

'This is the one who has been giving you problems?' she said.

'Another damned lawman,' Durant said. 'The one called Brand.'

He was still holding his revolver, the muzzle unwavering as he watched Brand closely.

Seraphina stood, moving to stand a few feet from Brand. She studied him, her gaze moving over his face and down his body.

'It would be interesting to find out more about him.'

'We will,' Durant said.

Dubois gave a gentle laugh. 'I don't think Seraphina was meaning that kind of information,' he said. 'She's more likely to be interested in his physical prowess.'

The woman glanced at him. 'There are times, Julienne, when you surprise even me.'

'Unfortunately,' Dubois said, 'we are

unable to linger. Your dear brother wants us back at the house. To help him with Buckman. We are to take the men with us. Just leave a couple here to back Durant while he deals with these two.'

'You think I need help?' Durant said, a scowl on his hard face.

'No point taking any chances,' Seraphina said. 'As soon as you're done here the bodies can be given to the bayou. Only this time make it happen.'

Dubois went out through the door and when he came back he informed them the casino had been cleared and closed. Seraphina turned and joined him.

'A shame we didn't get to know each other, Jason Brand,' she said. 'Too late now.'

'Maybe you can work your voodoo and bring me back from the dead.'

For a moment her face hardened as she stared at him.

'You shouldn't make fun of such things. It might be a mistake.'

'Story of my life. I make mistakes all

the time . . . but up to now I seem to walk away.'

'*Son of a bitch*,' Durant said and lashed out with the hefty revolver, catching Brand across the side of the head.

The blow put Brand on his knees, the room fading and seeming to sway in his eyes. When he was able to focus again he was alone in the room with Durant and Lyle Kelso.

Durant's big hands were wrapped around Lyle Kelso's neck, cruelly digging in the young policeman's flesh. Kelso was choking, his face suffused with blood, eyes bulging from their sockets. Durant shook the slim body like a dog with a rat. His revolver was jammed behind his leather belt.

'This the one you want?' Durant said. 'One of Noonan's tame coppers. Well, mister, you found him.' He chuckled. 'Only you left it too long.'

He increased his hold on Kelso's neck, the thick fingers buried deep in the flesh. Kelso's tongue bulged from

100

between his lips and a low breath of air came from his mouth.

'*Too damn late* . . . ' Durant whispered.

He squeezed a final time and Brand heard the crunch of bone. Kelso twitched a final time. Durant swung him aside, releasing his hold and Kelso's slack body was thrown across the room, striking the wall and sliding down in a lifeless sprawl.

'See, I let him go,' Durant said.

He had a crooked grin on his face as he closed in on Brand. The big man flexed his massive fists. His whole attitude suggested he was about to enjoy what was coming.

'You want me to kill you quick too, or make you suffer a while?'

Brand kept quiet as he sized the man up. There was no doubt Durant was big and hard. What Brand needed to know was the man's fighting potential. Was he skilled? Or did he simply depend on his massive bulk and an ability to take punishment? There was no doubt he was built to take it. Brand was going to find out. Durant was between him and the door, so one way or another Brand was going to have to fight his way through.

'I figured you would be dead already,' Durant said. 'Didn't expect you would last this long. But you reached the end of the line with me, lawdog. I don't figure to let you walk out of here. They'll have to carry you out . . . what's left of you . . . '

The man liked to talk. He was the kind who felt himself untouchable. Able to play his game by using his mouth.

Brand recalled what his instructor, Kito, had told him many times.

Let your opponent waste his time on chatter. You must concentrate on finding his weakness. Use it against him and do not throw away your chances. Use your strength to its best advantage and take your fight to him . . .

Brand understood one of his strengths would be his speed. His agility to move in fast, deliver, then draw back before

Durant could respond. He was going to have to overcome the knock to his head Durant had delivered because the man was working himself up to a killing mood.

Brand pushed upright, stepping away from the wall without hesitation, launching left and right jabs, his fists smacking against Durant's broad nose. He heard it break under the second blow, blood starting to stream down Durant's face and drip from his chin. The moment he struck Brand stepped away, out of the reach of Durant's large hands. Durant snorted, shaking his head as he absorbed the blows. Hard as he was the extreme pain made him pause. Brand followed through, slamming in hard punches to Durant's stomach, then changed direction, punching in at the man's exposed jaw. Durant's head snapped back and forth, a low growl coming from his mouth. His big, clenched fists snaked out, lashing out but meeting only thin air as Brand stepped away again, out of reach. Durant's frustration was making him reckless and he made a wild lunge forward that proved faster than Brand anticipated. Durant's swinging left fist connected with Brand's cheek, snapping his head to the side and giving Durant the chance to follow through, his right hand gripping Brand's shirt, fingers curling to take a solid hold. He yanked Brand close, eyes suddenly wide with anticipation as he swung his left backhand around in a powerful arc. It cracked against Brand's face and it felt as if his head was coming loose. In the next blurred seconds Brand knew he had to get clear before Durant beat him to a pulp.

'*Gonna beat the life out of you . . .*' Durant rasped, his words coming through the blood that was streaming across his mouth.

His hand swung again and Brand felt the numbing slam of it. Even in his pained moment he knew he needed to do something quickly, decisively, before Durant rendered him unconscious. He concentrated his efforts on Durant's lower body, his feet first. Brand slammed his boot heel down on Durant's right foot, putting his full force into the blow, repeating two, three times. The blows had the desired result, Durant's toes crushed to bloody pulp inside his leather boot and the big man gave a strangled cry. His attack on Brand briefly interrupted by the sudden pain, Durant's grip on his shirt slackened and Brand wrenched himself free, setting himself and drove the toe of his boot into the other's groin. He put all of his energy into the blow and it wrenched a howl of agony from the big man as he began to double over, clutching at his body. Brand caught hold of Durant's collar, pulling him forward and down. Brand's rising knee smashed into Durant's face and he felt the crunch of bone as it collapsed beneath the brutal force. As Durant began to slump forward, Brand stepped in close and encircled his thick neck in a tight embrace. The image of Kelso dangling from Durant's hands blurred his vision and he didn't hesitate as he applied a sudden twist. Felt Durant's neck flex. There was a soft crunch and Durant went totally limp. Brand held the lifeless bulk as Durant became, literally, a dead weight. He let the man slide from his grasp, stepped back to draw in a harsh breath.

The side of his head was becoming numb and Brand could feel fingers of blood running down his cheek where rings on Durant's fingers had scraped the skin. He took a moment to steady himself before he bent over Durant's body and retrieved the revolver from his belt. There was a short-barreled Colt jammed behind his broad leather belt. Brand checked the load. Five in the cylinder. He felt through the pockets of Durant's coat and found loose cartridges. He filled the empty chamber, dropped the other cartridges into a pocket.

Brand crouched beside Kelso's still form, shaking his head at the pointless loss of life. Another death on Lacroix's tally. It was time the list was closed, Brand decided.

He moved to the door and eased it open, checking the casino beyond. Two of Durant's crew were hunched over a baize covered table, concentrating on the hand of poker they were playing, too busy to be concerned over Durant's business. An opened bottle stood between them and a haze of tobacco smoke hung above their heads.

'*Hey*,' Brand called out and as they swiveled their heads, seeing him standing in the doorframe, they went for the pistols they wore.

The Colt in Brand's hand snapped into position and he put slugs into them before they had their weapons clear. The precision he displayed was tempered by the killing urge that rose in him. One man toppled from his chair, clutching his unused revolver, two .45 slugs in his chest. His partner caught a shot to the chest, a second slug slamming between his eyes and taking away a chunk of skull as it exited. He toppled over from his half-risen stance and crashed face down on the floor.

Brand remained where he was as he shucked out the spent casings and reloaded. He crossed the room and picked up one of the discarded revolvers. A longer barreled weapon, fully loaded. He tucked it behind his belt as he headed for the outer door. He spotted a .44–40 Henry repeater leaning against the wall and took that as well. A quick check under the barrel showed him the tubular magazine was full. That offered him sixteen shots. Brand worked the lever and as the rifle cocked it ejected a single load — *at least fifteen shots*, he corrected. He placed the revolver he was carrying behind his belt as well. A fully loaded rifle and a pair of ready handguns. If he couldn't handle whoever might stand against him with such an arsenal . . .

He went to the main door and opened it, checking the street. The Mardi Gras procession had moved on, leaving only a few stragglers. McCord had sent Brand to New Orleans to get to the bottom of the murder of Netta Delacort and the two other missing girls and that was what he was going to do. Any kind of diplomacy had already been pushed aside, so Brand figured it was time he meted out an *undiplomatic* solution. If that meant bringing some hellfire to the Crescent City, then that was how it was going to be.

★ ★ ★

Lacroix realized something was wrong when Julienne Dubois came into the study, his face pale. The Frenchman looked almost guilty, so Lacroix knew he was the bearer of bad news. Lacroix glanced across at his sister, a flick of a finger telling her to stay silent. As Dubois stepped through the door it closed behind him and Lacroix saw the man flinch.

'Julienne? Has someone broken the bank and we are out of money?'

'I wish it was something as simple,'

Dubois said. 'Clement just rode in from the city. The man, Brand, has escaped. He has killed three of our men.'

'I suspect there is more.'

'One of them was Durant.'

Lacroix met Seraphina's unflinching stare. She didn't have to speak. Her eyes spoke volumes and he knew she was angry.

'He snapped Durant's neck,' Dubois added. 'From what Clement found they fought. Durant lost. He killed the young police officer but failed to do the same with Brand.'

'Then we must make certain he does not kill any more of us,' Lacroix said.

Seraphina broke her silence. 'You believe it will be that easy?'

'He is only a man. He is not protected.'

'Then give him to me,' Seraphina said. 'My power will defeat him and I will bring him to his knees for you, brother. It will be my vengeance for Durant.'

'Let her do this, Victor,' Dubois said.

'Let her deal with this outsider while we proceed with the others. Buckman is wavering. We are so close now. To fail at this point would be a crime . . . '

Lacroix considered the point. He glanced at Seraphina. She returned his gaze, standing and crossing to his desk and resting her hands on the polished surface.

'Let me use *my* people. They can move around the city easily and with Mardi Gras in full swing they will not be noticed.'

'Ahh, your *followers*,' Dubois said, a suggestion of mockery in his voice.

Seraphina maintained her aloof expression. 'Still an unbeliever, Julienne. All the time you have spent here and you refuse to accept.'

'It is that I have my doubts, *ma chéri*.'

'Seraphina,' Lacroix said, 'our friend here is only driven by his quest for material gain. If he can see it and touch it then he is happy. Especially if what he seeks is in the form of gold and banknotes. Allow him his need for the material world.'

'Does that make me a bad person?' Dubois said. 'After all, Victor, it is why you employ me. To add to your own wealth. Am I wrong?'

Lacroix smiled because the Frenchman was correct. He had hired Dubois based on his ruthless and efficient managerial skills. Within the first couple of months he had turned around the overall take of Lacroix's gambling enterprises. Dubois ran the games without fear or favor and anyone who tried to fleece the tables was dealt with severely.

Lacroix was more than satisfied with the way Dubois operated. *The Creole Queen* had a solid reputation in the gambling community of New Orleans, with Dubois garnering the bulk of the praise. He sat back, content to watch the size of his bank balance rise on a regular basis. He understood Dubois' meticulous attention to the financial success of *The Creole Queen*. Lacroix had offered him a percentage of the take on top of his salary, so the more the casino made, the larger was his remuneration. It was an arrangement that benefitted them both. And as well as the money Lacroix received he was able to indulge his private interests.

As Dubois had stated, he was not interested in that side of Lacroix's dealings. His world revolved around the gaming tables, while Lacroix indulged himself, along with his sister, in an altogether separate life. Dubois knew little about it apart from it having something to do with local superstition. He had heard vague murmurings concerning voodoo and Creole traditions of witchcraft. Dubois had no interest in that. He viewed it as something out of the dark ages. Had heard it described as *mumbo-jumbo* nonsense. Knowing Lacroix's involvement in the cult and the serious intent he displayed where it was concerned Dubois refrained from anything controversial in the presence of the man and his sister. Of the two it was Seraphina the Frenchman was wary of. There was an aura around her that actually made him uneasy. The penetrating expression in her cold, dark eyes and the way she focused her gaze on him. Dubois had a genuine distrust of Seraphina. If there was any truth in the suggestion she was involved in unearthly pursuits Dubois wanted as little contact with her as he could. He distanced himself from her as much as possible, preferring the real world of the casino and the gambling. That was enough to hold Dubois' interest. What Lacroix and Seraphina got up to outside *The Creole Queen* was their affair. He wanted none of it.

With her brother's apparent say so the young woman took control.

'You can return to your gaming tables and your dice, Julienne,' she said soothingly. 'I will handle this man Brand. And he will soon vanish from our lives.'

'In a puff of colored smoke I

presume,' Dubois said, unable to resist a parting quip.

The thin smile on Seraphina's lips faded as Dubois left, quietly closing the door behind him.

'*One day*,' she said. 'One day I will take his head. Victor, I do not like that damned *cochon*.'

'My dear, it is not entirely required to *like* someone because they are in your employ. I must admit there are times his manner irritates, but that has to be weighed against the benefits of his skills. Julienne is most adept at his job and I cannot fault him. He runs the casino and brings in considerable amounts. Which you must accept is worth putting up with the man's presence.'

'You have a forgiving nature, brother. Far in excess than I.'

Lacroix was not going to argue that. His sister had a volatile temper and was capable of lashing out with little regard to the outcome. That included the violence she used to maintain order if necessary. Seraphina had no hesitation in ordering her people to maim and kill if it would bring her the results she wanted.

Lacroix, to a lesser degree, fed off the age-old rituals and wielded the power it gave him. He admitted his influence was not as great as his sister's. He depended on more traditional means to get what he wanted. Not that he had experienced as much success lately. His own attempt to have the man, Brand, disposed of had failed and it had been Lacroix who had lost his own men when they had taken Brand to the bayou. He had turned the tables on them.

Rene.

Lupe.

Grande — the coach driver.

Three of them had taken Brand out to the bayou to feed him to the alligators. But *only* Brand had come back to the city.

As good as his people had been they proved to be no match for the man.

Seraphina had said little but Lacroix knew she was not impressed. He was secretly pleased she had stepped in to take control of the situation, leaving Lacroix to deal with more mundane affairs.

Like maintaining his hold over the three men in the group who were now so afraid of being exposed they were offering him anything he demanded.

Except for Cyrus Buckman who was close to breaking down. If he did he might do something reckless and expose Lacroix and his operation. The man needed to be silenced before he did. This would be something Lacroix *could* take care of himself, leaving Seraphina to handle Brand, Now that Jake Durant was dead, Lacroix would have to have one of his other men deal with Buckman. He would call on a colleague who would handle the matter and remove Buckman. This time there would be no mistake. The man he had in mind would complete the task with his usual efficiency.

* ★ ★ ★

Doc Marcellus tended to Brand's cuts and bruises before he made his way back to the police station and Noonan's office. The Inspector's face paled when Brand informed him about Lyle Kelso's death.

'Damn,' he said. 'That's going to be on my conscience.'

'Don, you can't carry the blame for every police officer who dies doing his job.'

Noonan pressed his hand to his shoulder. The wound was still giving him pain.

'I do have some news that might be of interest. One of the officers looking out for Kelso saw Cyrus Buckman. The man was on foot and heading for his house. My man followed him and when he went inside he returned here to let me know. I'd given orders that if any of the missing people were seen I was to be informed immediately.'

'How long ago was this?'

'Couple of hours now. I sent the officer back to stand watch. Name of Brenner.'

'It's time I had a little talk with our banker.'

'Brenner said when he saw Buckman he was in a terrible state. Unshaven, clothes in a mess. Don't be too hard on the man.'

Brand managed a mirthless smile. 'I promise not to be too hard on him. Don, you should be at home resting.'

'I was shot. One of my men has been killed and you have been pursued and generally knocked about, Jason. Do you think I'm about to sit by with my feet up?'

'Way you look I'd say it was the best thing you can do.'

'I feel so damned useless.'

'If you put it like that, Inspector Noonan, I already know the answer. Just promise me you've got a loaded revolver in your desk.'

'Two if truth be told. And they're both loaded.'

Brand pushed to his feet.

'Jason, be careful. We may have Lacroix on the defensive. If that's true he isn't about to give up easily.'

'Well that's going to make for an interesting time because the same thing has been said about me.'

As the office door closed behind Brand the New Orleans policeman considered the situation and decided Brand was ready to start turning the city on its head and to hell with whoever he upset doing it.

★ ★ ★

Earlier . . .

Cyrus Buckman's days as President of the bank were long and seemed to comprise of seemingly endless meetings with clients. When he had first established the bank, his importance excited him. He thrived on the challenge. The cut and thrust of his chosen profession. He was an important figure. He held power in his hands. People looked to him for advice, trusted him with their money, held him in great esteem.

And Buckman loved it. Loved every minute. He moved in the highest levels of New Orleans society. Without becoming fully aware as the years passed, his affinity to his life style began to wane. It came down on him on his forty-fifth birthday. The day he looked in his mirror and saw the aging face staring back at him. Only now did he realize how his life was passing him by. Oh, he had the power. The wealth. A fine house and possessions. With a shock he looked at himself and saw the middle-aged figure reflected in the glass. The distant eyes and the pale complexion. The image of a man who was lonely, with little in his life apart from . . .

In truth he had nothing. His work had dominated his life, leaving him little time to enjoy anything beyond the bank. No wife. No female companion. Middle-aged he lived with his sister

Eleanor, who he had cared for since their parents had passed away many years ago. She was happy in her role as his companion, as she called herself. Never one for looking beyond the four walls of the house. She arranged his domestic needs. Kept the big house in order. Cooked his meals and when he entertained, to maintain contacts, it was Eleanor who arranged the dinner parties for his guests. She was never more content than when she was doing these things and he let her look after him because it was convenient.

Now he took a long look at himself and the way his life was slipping by, and suddenly he found he saw nothing but emptiness. He did not enjoy what he saw and made a decision to change things.

Once a week Cyrus Buckman met two of his friends at the club they all belonged to. It was a gentlemen's club. Here they were able to gather to sample fine drinks and smoke expensive cigars while they talked. Mostly they talked business because, like Buckman, Coleman and Dalton, they had similarly dull lives outside their business dealings. In truth they had little else to talk about. It was, they decided, fortuitous when Victor Lacroix came into their lives. He had become a member of the club, buying his way in with a generous donation, and ingratiating himself with his favors. He quickly became a welcome figure in the club society and it was by no means a help that he owned and ran one of the most successful establishments on Bourbon Street that catered to the gamblers and womanizers of New Orleans.

Lacroix welcomed Buckman and his friends to *The Creole Queen* where the three men were able to indulge themselves in card games, roulette, and drink the chilled champagne served by the attractive hostesses. In the exclusive back room the gambling was select and the stakes were high. Only special guests were invited there, under the close supervision of Julienne Dubois. The Frenchman oversaw the proceedings, offering whatever the clientele wanted and it was on his say so that Lacroix was able to pick out players who held promise of bigger and better pickings.

Cyrus Buckman and his companions were ideal for *special* treatment. There was no denying their wealth. Buckman was the banker. Coleman a man of business with holdings in a number of prestigious New Orleans companies, and Dalton was President of a powerful land company. Between them they controlled immense wealth and had influence in the city.

As they became totally embroiled in Lacroix's offerings, becoming more under his control, he invited them to his out of town home, where they were able to let themselves go completely. They were also naive when it came to indulging in the vices Lacroix could offer. From the young women, and young men where Dalton was concerned, to liquor and beyond, to the baser indulgences they took to them with voracious appetites. Lacroix indulged them, encouraged them, promising discretion and urging them on to even greater excesses. The visits became regular, allowing the three to experience delights they never knew existed. And when they were fully immersed in the wanton fulfillments provided by Lacroix, before any kind of guilt began to creep in, they were enmeshed in the dark pleasures the man was offering them.

It was Lacroix's sister who was instrumental in wielding the power that entrapped Buckman and his friends. Her natural beauty, coupled with the sensual attraction of the mesmerizing voodoo power she displayed. In the shadowy, enshrouded displays of her skills, she held Buckman and his friends under her spell. In the shadowed labyrinth beneath the house Seraphina played them with her dark magic, assisted by her acolytes who followed her every word and gesture. Buckman and his friends, lulled by the wafting swirls of misty smoke issuing from the vessels placed around them and the cigarettes that were freely distributed — in fact opium — were taken from normality into the stupor-induced states that fogged their minds and allowed Seraphina to do what she wanted with them

★ ★ ★

Buckman dimly remembered the sweet smell of the cigarettes. The pleasing feeling that enveloped him as he inhaled. And the similar scent that rose from the smoldering dishes placed around the room. It was only later he realized the soporific sensation that enveloped him came from opium. It washed over him like a warm tide, gently distancing him from reality and spiraling away from the real world into . . .

. . . a place where troubles and worries vanished, leaving him drowsy, his will to resist vanishing. The room lost its harshness and he was cocooned in a gentling glow where he reclined in an enticing atmosphere and he saw Seraphina standing next to him, her lithe body naked, glistening as she came closer, the soft ripple of a drum beat echoing in rhythm to her teasing movements . . . Buckman retained enough of his senses to know this was not real . . . that the visions were in his mind . . . affected by the power of the drug . . . and the hands stroking his exposed flesh were part of his imagining . . . the fear flickered in the deeper recesses of his mind . . . the whole thing some fantasy conjured by Lacroix and his sister . . . and he had to break out from it before . . .

'No,' he called, his voice a faint whisper that battled against the hold of the drug. *'I will not be part of this. Let me go . . . let me go . . .'*

'But this is what you wanted,' Seraphina said. 'What you desired. Now it is too late to go back. You know how that girl died . . . because she

would no longer do what I asked . . .
you have seen the pictures . . . understood how it had to be because she
rejected me . . . not like the others who
gave you what you desired . . . '

'I had nothing to do with the death of
that girl. Nothing . . . this is all a
nightmare . . . something you made
happen to trick us . . . it is not magic
. . . it is all trickery . . . and you are just
a part of it all . . . a fake . . . nothing
but a charlatan . . . '

'Am I, Cyrus Buckman? Is this not
real? Now you have rejected me. Called
me a fake . . . is it so? We will see . . . '

In his mind Buckman fought the
images. He closed his ears to the
insistent sounds. Rejected the sensa-
tions that threatened to consume him.

Seraphina's image wavered, faded
and Buckman heard the sound of the
drums coming from the shadows
starting to grow quieter. But then he
had begun to choke as he breathed in
the smoky fumes. The sensation grew
stronger. It felt so real. As was the heat

reaching out to engulf his body. It seemed to ignite his clothing, burning through to blister his flesh. Buckman struggled to break out of the dream but found he was unable to raise his arms. He struggled, then realized his hands and arms were bound by cords, holding him spread-eagled on some cold marble slab that prevented him from helping himself. As he twisted his head back and forth, desperate to escape the increasing swell of the fire, and failing, he saw the face before his eyes.

Circled by the rising flames yet untouched it was the face and body of Seraphina Lacroix again. She was still naked as she leaned in closer, her hand appearing, a finger admonishing him.

'I said you would regret mocking me,' she whispered. 'Dismissing my powers with such arrogance, Cyrus. Now we shall witness who holds the truth. Who will become the victor.'

Her voice had a hollow tone to it. The words sliding out with a mocking sibilance.

Buckman felt the flesh of his face pulling tight over his bones as the flames threatened to draw him in. He could smell hair scorching. His clothing smoldering.

It was as if it was real.

Not a dream.

But it had to be a dream, he told himself. The effects of the drugs Seraphina had tricked him into taking.

Seraphina's image vanished as quickly as it had appeared and Buckman found himself alone again, misty shadows coiling around him.

He was still in the cellar. In the house where he had been all evening. Seraphina's threats were simply that, he told himself. The boastful threats of a woman not used to having her so-called power challenged. And everything he was experiencing was a figment of his own imagination.

It had to be.

It couldn't be real.

Could it?

He called out. Then realized he couldn't even hear his own voice. He yelled the words but there was only silence. The beginnings of panic nibbled at his consciousness.

This had to be something conjured by Seraphina?

She had drugged him so that these images were no more than hallucinations. Yet if they were they damn well hurt. The heat was all around him now and the temperature had risen to the point where Buckman knew he had to do something, even if it was only to wake up.

He tugged at his bound wrists, feeling a degree of slack, the rope slick against his sweating flesh.

I can do this, he told himself. *I can do this.*

He spread the fingers of his right hand and willed his mind to banish the burning images around him. He fought to reach into the depths of his conscious thoughts, seeking some solid thing to allow him to draw out of

Seraphina's dream world and let him touch reality.

At first there was nothing.

Then he felt the lip of the altar. The cool marble, and he rubbed his palm across the sharp edge, deliberately forcing his hand against it, feeling the slightly ragged edge tugging at his flesh. Buckman forced his palm harder against the marble, felt the edge break his skin. He maintained the action, sawing back and forth until he felt sudden pain as the marble sliced his flesh. He knew he had gashed his palm, and the sudden surge of keen pain jolted his senses. He felt the blood run across his hand and kept on dragging his hand across the marble . . .

. . . Buckman became aware of a subtle change in his surroundings. The darkness receded and he sensed himself at ease again, as if some challenging sensory effect had been reduced. The flames disappeared. The heat and the swirl of smoke began to withdraw, and though he still felt uncomfortable, the strong sense of foreboding was lessening. His flesh and his clothing were whole. Untouched by the fire. When he raised his head he saw Seraphina standing at the base of the marble plinth, staring down at him, face taut with barely repressed anger and a degree of frustration because he had broken the grip of her actions over him.

'No more,' he said forcibly. 'I will not allow you to control me.'

Her face, once beautiful, had become ugly and she glared at him with what he could only define as a mix of bitterness and rage.

'I can do what I desire . . . '

Buckman sat up, realizing the cords that had seemed to bind him had vanished. He could feel the sharp, pulsing pain in his hand where he had torn it against the marble. Blood was running from the gash freely now, dripping from his fingers. The pain had drawn his mind from the cloying seduction of the opium, allowing him to draw on rational thought.

'Get away from me . . . away . . . damn you, woman . . .'

He wrenched himself to one side, sliding across the slab until he toppled, falling to the cold earth of the cellar, fighting the lethargy that had gripped him, aware that he had to escape from this place. Had to get out. Away. Back into the real world.

As he dragged himself to his feet, leaning against the marble slab, staring about him, he realized he was by himself. Seraphina had vanished and he was alone in the shadowed cellar. Buckman stumbled across the uneven floor, seeing shapes emerge in the faint light that found its way through gaps in the outer wall. He moved towards the light, clumsy footed, his whole body trembling and aching. He came to the wooden door set in the cellar wall, the warped timber letting in streaks of daylight. Weak as he was Buckman thrust his body against the door. It gave but resisted his initial attempts to break it open. With a strength borne of desperation, Buckman drove his shoulder against the door again and again, sobbing with the effort, ignoring the pain from his shoulder. The driving force behind his efforts was the fear Seraphina might appear again, using the force of will to subdue him. He concentrated his pounding against the door and it suddenly swung open on creaking hinges. The suddenness of the action pitched Buckman forward, falling to his knees as the cold chill of air struck him and he was aware of falling rain. He lifted his head, feeling the cold strike him, helping to drive away some of the opium fumes that still fogged his mind.

He had to get away from this place. Back to the real world. To the city where he would be among normal people. In truth, he had no choice. If he stayed here he would die. Lacroix and Seraphina could not allow him to tell what he had learned. So regardless of the danger he had to get away.

Buckman moved with a speed that

surprised himself. He knew it was fear of being caught that added to his flight. Stumbling, falling and dragging himself upright again, he moved along the side of the house, ignoring the cold and the discomfort. If he was caught minor things like rain and the hurt that racked his body would be nothing compared to what Lacroix would do to him.

When he reached the end of the building, leaning against the stonework, Buckman peered around the corner and saw the wide open drive in front of him.

A buggy and two-horse team stood patiently waiting, heads down against the falling rain. At first he thought he was imagining the sight. A second look convinced him it was no apparition. Buckman didn't hesitate. He pushed himself forward, gaining enough speed to take him across the circular drive and up to the buggy. He forced himself to stare directly ahead, convinced that if he didn't see anyone they might not materialize. Barely able to believe his luck he reached the buggy and dragged himself on board, picking up the reins as he settled on the seat. He pulled on the reins, dragging the heads of the team around, flicking their backs with the whip he plucked from the side holder. The pair of horses broke into motion and Buckman slapped the reins across their backs, raising his voice to yell at them despite the risk of being overheard.

The buggy rocked from side to side as Buckman cracked the whip over their heads, wheels sliding and he almost lost his grip on the reins. Despite that he held on and saw the open gates in front of him. He also saw an arm-waving figure step into view. The man held a shotgun in one hand but was intent on halting Buckman's approach. Ignoring the terror rising in his throat Buckman refused to back down. He urged the team on faster and the gateman had to leap aside as the buggy bore down on him. Buckman kept up the pace, turning the team in a slithering curve onto the road that would take him back towards New Orleans.

Trees and bushes flashed by on either side. The sheeting rain stung his face. Buckman kept the team on a headlong rush, not daring to look back in case he was being pursued. His logical mind told him Lacroix would not follow in case his people were recognized. He would want to keep matters secret. Even so Buckman knew that one way or another the man would engineer some kind of retribution. He had a need to keep his dark secrets just that — secret. So any strike against Buckman would need to be kept behind closed doors.

Buckman was glad now he had managed to persuade his sister to leave the city. He wanted her out of harm's way. What he had gotten himself involved in had nothing to do with Eleanor. She was completely naïve when it came to the dark goings on and that was how Buckman wanted it to stay. With her out of the way he no longer had to worry about her safety.

All he had to do was attempt to put things right. He had allowed himself to be drawn into Lacroix's evil games so it was down to him to get himself out . . . how he had no idea at the moment. First he needed to get back to town. Give himself time to think. To decide how he would go about saving himself.

He slowed the buggy as he reached the outskirts of the city and drove at a slower pace, negotiating the near-deserted streets. The rain had forced most people indoors so he abandoned the buggy at the first opportunity and walked the rest of the way to his home. It took him some time as he wearily tramped the remainder of the journey. He was close to collapse by the time he reached the house and let himself in. When he closed the door and leaned against it, the bone-deep tiredness engulfed him.

He was soaked, his body ached, and in the empty silence of his house the memories came flooding back. He tried to fight them off but in his sheer exhaustion he failed. With a tortured moan he slumped to the floor and lay in a stupor. Without knowing it, he fell into a deep sleep. Yet in that sleep he was plagued by the visions of what had happened and how he had become so enmeshed in Victor Lacroix's world . . . it had happened so gradually that he was unaware how he was being manipulated . . . by the time he realized it was too late . . . the trap had been sprung and Buckman and his friends were well and truly caught . . .

. . . *Cyrus Buckman lived in a wealthy part of New Orleans. Every house in the area was large, standing on large plots and boasted multiple rooms. Buckman had always felt himself privileged to be where he was. He held a respected position in one of the city's most prestigious banks — in fact he owned the bank. But right now he might as well have been a beggar on the street. Since his involvement with Victor Lacroix and his sister, Seraphina, his cozy world had started to fall apart.*

What had seemed an enticing diversion from the staid world of banking had become dark and at times terrifying.

At first the secret meetings, alongside his two friends — Jerome Coleman and Henry Dalton — men of stature and business like himself — had taken an unexpected turn. The debauched entertainment, the unrestrained sexual encounters, that had excited and overwhelmed them, gradually took on a shadowy and sensual turn. By then, deeply involved in the insidious practices of Lacroix and his sister, Buckman and his companions were open targets for what was to follow. There was little they could do to counter the open threats of exposure. Lacroix had, simply, blackmailed them. During the frenzied episodes, senses dulled by copious drinking and the use of opium that Seraphina used to lull them, Buckman and his friends had been caught by Lacroix's concealed photographer. When he had shown them the results, with the implied threat to

141

publicly show the photographs, the three men had been too shocked to do anything but submit to his demands.

Seraphina Lacroix had openly flaunted herself at them, forcing them to recall what they had been involved in during their intoxicated and opium drugged states. Her devotion to the voodoo arts, which she had employed to seduce them into their compliant conditions, were implicit in her demands that they remain silent on what they had seen and heard. She used the enticement of her beliefs and her strength to subdue them. She had a strong following in the local Creole beliefs in the power of voodoo and Buckman and his friends were caught up in the craft. Seraphina used her black magic to good effect. Her acolytes were enslaved. They entered into the spirit of the sessions, in awe at her magic powers, the hold she had over anyone who came close to her — and that included Buckman and his friends, though for different reasons. The thrill of the sexual encounters and the way in which their heightened senses gave them feelings long since dormant.

It was only later they realized that images they had thought were imagined turned out to be real. The rituals came back to them as the hallucinatory feelings faded and Buckman, of them all, took on his shoulders what he realized were true images.

In the semi-darkness, enveloped in the grip of Seraphina's magic, they had seen and heard the frenzied activities, taking part in many of the rituals themselves. It had been only in the cold light of reasoning, with the return to reality, did the enormity of what they had witnessed strike home. That awareness had crashed down on them, the bitter truth that they had been witness to the death of the young woman, Netta Delacort, they had imagined was part of the fantasy woven by Seraphina's voodoo-induced performances. Yet despite the misgivings, they returned each time Lacroix and

143

Seraphina extended an invitation, coaxed and drawn back into the dark fantasies that had them in its grip.

When reality finally dawned they were, to a man, too far entangled to walk away. With all that Lacroix had on them the group were forced to choose between acquiescing to his demands or being exposed. If they admitted to what they had been involved in it would have meant public humiliation for them and their families, with the prospect of criminal charges and possible prison sentences. The price Lacroix demanded for his silence was substantial portions of their business holdings and even financial offerings. It was out-and-out extortion, with Lacroix's sister adding to the threat with her voodoo curses that she had burned into the susceptible minds of the victims during her elaborate ceremonies. Ridden with guilt and plagued by the physical threats, Buckman and his two associates, were wracked with premonitions of terror and monstrous retribution.

Cyrus Buckman was the first to break. The death of the young woman preyed on his mind, becoming stronger as time passed. His will to resist crumbled and he degenerated into a shambling wreck. His sleep was disturbed and his waking hours no better. He understood the penalty if he admitted to what he had been involved in, yet his attempt to suppress the knowledge he carried inside his head threatened to tear his world apart. As the head of the bank he owned he was able to step aside and allow his staff to run the business without his presence. He needed time away from the bank as he tried, not too successfully, to decide how to handle the darkness overwhelming his very existence. Shutting himself away in his study at home and refusing to face his increasingly concerned sister, Buckman began to drink heavily in an attempt to ease the troubles in his increasingly tortured mind . . . but even in his befuddled state he found himself unable to resist the lure offered by

Lacroix and his sister . . . and he went back for more . . .

★   ★   ★

Lucero *Doctor* Vallejo. Six-foot-six tall. A lean, almost skeletal, figure. Skin so dark as to be near black. A shaven skull. His eyes bright with a maniacal brightness. The man moved with little visible effort, coming and going with the effortless ease of a shadow. His past history was replete with contradictions and even Lacroix didn't have the full story. Not that he really cared about that. He employed Vallejo for his murderous skills. The somberly dressed assassin's ability to carry out any contract he accepted was what interested Lacroix. He had used Vallejo on a number of previous occasions and the killer's success rate spoke for itself.

When Lacroix sent for him, dispatching one of his underlings to contact the man, Vallejo had shown up at the house within the hour. When he left, less than a half-hour later, he carried Lacroix's money in his pocket and the information about Cyrus Buckman in his head. The conversation Lacroix had had with the man had been conducted in a couple of dozen words. Alone once again in his study Lacroix sat back knowing he would have no more problems with Buckman.

The man was as good as dead.

★ ★ ★

Buckman had roused from his tortured slumber, cold and weak. It had taken him a long time to climb to his feet, feeling the chill of the unheated house. Beyond the windows the rain was still falling. He leaned against the doorframe, shivering and realized he was still wearing his damp clothing. Somehow he managed to climb the stairs and in his bedroom he removed the sodden clothes, dressing in fresh ones. At some point he caught sight of himself in his dressing mirror and almost recoiled at the image.

Dark shadows under his eyes. His face blotchy and unshaven. His hair wild and tangled. As a usually fastidious man who dressed well, seeing himself in such a state shocked him immensely.

He left the room, stumbled down the stairs and made for his study. He filled a thick tumbler with bourbon and downed it in swift gulps, almost choking on the liquor. He immediately refilled the glass and took the bottle with him as he crossed the study and sank into one of the heavy leather armchairs facing the window behind his large desk.

Buckman sat in solitary melancholy and watched as rain sluiced down the glass. Now he wrestled with his conscience, unsure what to do. Admit what he had been involved in and face the real possibility of prison — a prospect that filled him with horror. How could he, Cyrus Buckman, be locked up in one of those terrible places? He knew enough about incarceration to believe he would never survive such a place. And in admitting his part in the deviant world of Victor Lacroix, his reputation would be in tatters. There would be little support from those who knew him. The crème of New Orleans society would distance themselves, condemning what he had done, and when it came out — as it surely would — that he had been part of the murder of an innocent girl from a well-to-do family — his fate would be surely sealed. Buckman's world would disintegrate in front of his eyes. It would be over, with no going back. And how would he be able to face the families of those missing girls? He thought of Netta Delacort. He knew the girl's father and the realization he was involved with the people who had murdered her sickened him.

He gripped the thick tumbler, filled with more bourbon. He had already consumed a number of drinks and raised the tumbler to his lips once more, hand trembling as he considered one option open to him.

Death would release him from the torment. Yet even as he considered it, he knew he could not take his own life. He had always seen suicide as a coward's way out. Buckman could not take pain. Even the slightest. To inflict it on himself was beyond his comprehension.

So he sat and stared out of his window, unsure where his life was going, and completely at a loss as to what he could do about it.

The decision was made for him a short time later, the need to make choices taken from him as his home received two visitors.

One came to question him.

The other to kill him.

★　★　★

The cab dropped Brand outside the house and the driver settled back to wait. The city lay behind them, the area a collection of large, expensive houses all standing in their own grounds. This, Brand decided, was where the elite of New Orleans lived. Just before Brand left the police station he had pulled on an oilskin topcoat Noonan had borrowed for him. It repelled the downpour as he approached the house. The fall was heavy and he could feel it drumming against his hat.

A similarly garbed figure was watching the house. He started forward as Brand approached the house.

'Constable Brenner?'

The policeman acknowledged.

'And who would you be?'

'Jason Brand. Inspector Noonan said you were watching the house. Has Buckman showed himself since he first arrived?'

'You'd be the man from Washington.'

'Hell, my secret seems to be getting around a sight too freely.'

'In New Orleans it's hard to keep any secrets for long. Now there's been no sight or sound of Buckman since he showed up.'

'Will you wait around while I go and have a talk with him? Keep an eye out.'

'Expecting trouble?'

'I always *expect*.'

Brand made his way up the path to the front door. His survival instinct made him open the coat so he had access to the shoulder-holstered Colt special he was wearing. It was a normal reaction as far as Brand was concerned. In his business second chances were few and far between, so despite his visit to Cyrus Buckman's home being an information search, Brand figured caution was needed.

He moved up the wide stone steps to the heavy front door, ready to knock. In her distressed condition Eleanor Buckman had chosen to stay in the city, with an old friend for a time when Buckman had asked. There were no servants in residence at the house, so Cyrus Buckman should be alone.

The sudden shrill scream coming

from inside the house made all the difference . . .

★ ★ ★

. . . it was the faint reflection in the rain-streaked glass that warned Buckman. Even in his semi-stupor from the bourbon he knew he was no longer alone. That someone was behind him. The tall, dark figure looming over the back of his chair clutched a long-bladed knife that was already making a down stroke. Buckman dropped his whiskey tumbler as he pulled his body forward. The blade, aimed for the side of his throat, caught him between the shoulder blades, cutting through his clothing and gouging his flesh. Pain flared, blood flowed and Buckman let out a high scream as he wrenched himself away from his assailant, desperate to get away from his would be killer. In his haste he stumbled, dropping to his knees, then attempted to climb to his feet.

Lacroix's hired assassin — *Doctor*

Vallejo — reached out and manhandled the chair aside and took a long stride forward, the blade of his knife seeking his target again. He needed to end this quickly. Before anything could happen to put him in any danger. He was used to his kills going without any kind of problem, so Buckman avoiding what should have been a fatal blow had taken Vallejo by surprise. He lashed out with his knife again, this time making a deep cut across the back of Buckman's neck, from one side to the other, the razor edge going in deep. Blood spurted from the wound yet the man refused to go down, staggering to his feet despite the heavy flow of blood from the wounds. He managed to turn his body, arms flaying wildly and his left hand caught Vallejo across the side of his head. The blow stung and caught Vallejo in mid stride. He faltered for a couple of seconds before recovering and prepared to launch himself forward again.

Behind him the door to the study crashed open, swinging wide and Vallejo threw a glance over his shoulder at the disturbance . . .

* * *

. . . the house door opened freely and Brand went inside. He picked up noise coming from behind a door to his left. He reached it in three long strides. Heard the crash of a piece of furniture being thrust aside. He paused at the door, raised his right foot and kicked the door wide, moving into the room without pause.

Two men.

One he took to be Cyrus Buckman, struggling to remain on his feet, face deathly white as he threw up both hands to ward off . . .

. . . a tall, skinny black man with a bloodied knife raised in his right hand, ready to strike again. With Brand's entrance the man glanced back over his shoulder, lips peeled away from his teeth in a snarl of defiance.

Brand didn't even pause. He raised

155

the Colt, hammer back, and held it on the man. He tripped the trigger, the .45 caliber crashing out its shot. The lead slug slammed into Vallejo's right shoulder, going all the way through and knocking the assassin off balance, turning him so he was facing Brand. Before Vallejo could recover Brand fired twice more, each slug placed deliberately on target. The second shot was into Vallejo's body, tunneling through to his spine, severing it and as the man started to fall Brand triggered his final shot. It slammed into the shaven skull, sinking in and terminating the brain function. Vallejo went to the floor without a sound.

Brand put the Colt away as he crossed to where Buckman had slumped over his desk, clinging to it and as he turned Brand saw the blood streaming from the deep cut across the back of his neck and the wound between his shoulders. He assisted the moaning man into the chair he righted, then ran from the room and to the front door. Rain was drifting inside.

Brenner, alerted by the shots, was halfway up the path.

'Got a hurt man in here,' Brand called out. 'You know Doctor Marcellus?'

'I know him.'

'Send the cab man. Tell him there's a badly knifed man needs his help. *Go*. Make it quick.'

Brenner nodded and ran to the cab as Brand turned back into the house. He spotted the door to the kitchen and went there, searching for cloth he could use for bandages. He found clean kitchen towels, picked them up and returned to Buckman's study.

The man was close to being unconscious, blood having soaked his clothes clear down to his waist. Brand turned him sideways and used the towels to wad over the severe, wide-open deep gash across his neck. He was unable to stop the blood flow, the towel quickly sodden. Brand used a second and third towel to hold in place, his own hands becoming soaked as the blood flow continued.

He became aware of Buckman staring at him, his gaze unsteady. The man laid one of his hands on Brand's arm, his mouth moving soundlessly.

'I sent for Doc Marcellus. Try to hang on.'

'I have to tell you . . . now before it's too late. We were so foolish. We did terrible things. Let them draw us in . . . and we knew what had been done . . . but we were too weak to stop by then . . . those poor girls . . . what they did to them . . . '

Brand could feel the hot blood streaming across his hands. There was nothing he could do and he knew that no matter how fast Marcellus was in coming, even he wouldn't be able to do anything now.

'Damned foolish men. All of us. We thought it would be exciting . . . secret and dangerous . . . but we just let it happen . . . the sex and the opium and the drinking . . . no harm but then we were in so deep there was no way we could escape. When we realized about the girls . . . what would happen if we were exposed . . . we fell for their lies . . . the threats . . . those pictures they took of us . . . and then the blackmail. They promised as long as we did what they wanted they would keep our secrets. God, it was such a mess. No way out if we wanted to stay free. Not exposure. Not prison. Everyone knowing what we had been doing . . . the shame . . . for our families . . . businesses ruined . . . I . . . '

Brand felt the man shivering as he began to slip into a state of unconsciousness. Buckman's hand closed even tighter against Brand's arm, fingers gripping painfully. He knew the man was close to death, but he needed one more thing from him.

Confirmation on who was behind it all.

Brand knew, but he needed to hear it from Buckman himself.

'Buckman . . . Cyrus . . . who was it?

The names, man. I need to hear it from you.'

Buckman stared at him for what seemed an eternity. The shivering stopped and it was as if he was already gone. Then his other hand reached across to clutch at Brand's arm.

'*Victor Lacroix*. He's the one. With his sister, Seraphina. They're in it together. Look in his house . . . in the cellars . . . I think you'll find the missing girls there . . . and my friends . . . they may still be alive . . . '

★ ★ ★

When Doctor Regis Marcellus arrived twenty minutes later, with the cab driver on his heels he stepped into the study and found the man called Vallejo dead on the floor. Cyrus Buckman was slumped in a seat, his blood soaked body still and cold. His blood had run down across the seat and pooled on the carpeted floor beneath him.

Brand, his hands and wrists still

covered in drying blood, was leaning back in a chair, a bottle in one hand and a half-filled tumbler in the other. He stared across the room at Marcellus, shaking his head.

'Couldn't save him, Doc. Hell, it's easy to take a life. Not so easy to save one.'

He swallowed the rest of the whiskey and refilled the tumbler. His face was expressionless, eyes bleak and Marcellus knew better than to force the issue.

Marcellus inspected Buckman's body. His professional eye taking in the terrible, deep slash across his neck and the stab wound in his back. He turned to glance down at Vallejo, seeing the bullet wounds and the damage to the man's skull where Brand's .45 slug had taken it apart.

'This is getting out of hand,' Marcellus said. 'Don't you agree?'

'No argument from me. After what Buckman told me there's no question.'

'He spoke to you?'

'I guess you could call it his confession.'

'You have my attention,' Marcellus said. He glanced back at Vallejo's sprawled body. 'I take it he was more than a burglar?'

'I don't think he came to steal. More likely to silence Buckman before he gave too much away.'

'I'm the first to admit New Orleans can be a rough town, but this is all getting beyond me, Jason. Did Cyrus name names?'

Brand drained his tumbler. 'He told me what I needed to know.'

'Lacroix?'

'And his sister.'

'*Seraphina?*'

'All to do with her damned voodoo games and the blackmail of Buckman and his friends.'

'Netta Delacort? The missing girls?'

'Down to the brother and sister's sick games. A Creole Curse that's gone too far. Lacroix can't walk away from this now. Buckman had taken enough. He couldn't hide it any longer. I reckon he was ready to give Lacroix up to the law but he waited too long. Allowed Lacroix to send in his assassin to shut the man up. Buckman thought the kidnapped girls could still be in the house.'

'So what happens now?'

Brand looked across at him and Marcellus didn't need to ask further.

'I had better call the undertaker. Have him move the bodies. Damn, this is going to be hard on Eleanor. Poor woman has already had to deal with Cyrus and his problems. Now this.'

Brand put the tumbler aside and stood.

'You need any backup, Doc, I'll be around.'

'Take care,' Marcellus said. 'Jason, just make sure whoever is behind this doesn't get away with it.'

Brand's smile was all the more chilling because it failed to show any kind of humor. He stared at Marcellus for a few seconds, as he came to his decision.

'*They won't,*' he said. '*You have my word on that.*'

★ ★ ★

Now.

He left his rented horse tied in the deep foliage a good half-mile from Lacroix's estate, moving in on foot. The rain was still sluicing from a heavy sky as he worked his way to the high stone wall that encircled the big house.

After leaving Marcellus and returning to his hotel Brand cleaned up and dressed in a dark outfit of shirt and pants and armed himself with his holstered Colt. From the hotel he sought out a livery stable and rented a horse and rode out of New Orleans in the direction of Lacroix's estate.

Brand's approach to the place seemed to go unobserved. It wasn't the first time he had been forced to make a silent approach. His main concern was making certain Lacroix didn't have any of his people patrolling the outside

164

of the estate. He saw nothing. Heard nothing. It was possible Lacroix felt confident enough not to need outside guards. Even so Brand took his time. It would have been so easy to allow his confidence to let him make mistakes. From his recent dealings with Lacroix's men he understood the man had no qualms when it came to dealing with anyone he felt a threat. The man's position in New Orleans had given him a feeling of invulnerability. He *knew* people who would provide him with backup. *Influential* people. Brand didn't let himself worry too much over that. He was operating with the approval of the one man who held influence that would override anything Lacroix could hold up.

The President of the United States.

As far as Brand was concerned he needed no other backup.

Except perhaps Frank McCord. To be honest Brand would have rather gone against the President than face McCord's disapproval.

165

He crouched in the shadowed confines of the dense undergrowth. Surveying the high barrier the wall presented he hoped there would be an easier way in. Off to his left the wall snaked its way to the high metal gates closing off the grounds.

Faint sound reached his ears. Brand saw a figure moving along the outer wall, in his direction. The man wore a glistening poncho and had a Henry rifle cradled loosely in his arms. He moved with the air of a man who had trodden this particular path many times. Too many times it seemed by the bored way he was walking, barely taking notice of his surroundings. When he drew level with the gates the man paused to peer through the bars, most likely wishing he was inside the house rather than tramping around it in the rain.

Keep coming, feller.

The man did, approaching the spot where Brand crouched in the dense growth at the foot of the wall. Slipping his Colt from the holster Brand reversed it. He was going to have to employ it as a club. There was no way he could risk a shot so close to the house.

The closer the guard got the louder his boot steps. Brand saw his shadow fall across the ground and held himself motionless as the figure reached and passed him. As soon as the man's back was to him Brand rose, swift and silent. His left hand reached out to pull the man's hat from his head, his right bringing the heavy revolver down across the exposed skull. Brand hit hard, withholding nothing. The solid thud of the strike was followed by a short grunt as the man stumbled, knees giving way. Brand followed him down, striking a second time. The guard's solid bulk thudded against the ground, rifle trapped beneath his body. He jerked once then laid still, blood starting to bleed from the ragged gash in his skull.

Brand moved to the gates and slipped through. He started along the hard-packed drive that led in the direction of the big house. There were willowy trees and high ferns lining the drive. Brand used them as cover on his approach to the house, his eyes taking in the classical lines of the building with its high frontage, intricate ironwork edging the verandahs that showed at the many windows. The main entrance was decorated by a stone-columned porch affair. The high front doors were painted in a deep red, furnished with gleaming copper handles and hinges. The antebellum architecture was reminiscent of a faded era that still held sway in parts of the south.

Brand reached as close as he could without exposing himself. The approach drive ended in a wide circular area directly fronting the house. There was ample space for carriages and buggies to turn about.

Brand waited. Studying the layout around the big house and finding himself intrigued by the armed men. What did Lacroix have that required such a level of security. He sat back against the thick trunk of the tree. The question in his mind asked — was Lacroix guarding against someone getting inside his home, or preventing someone getting out? The first thing that came into his mind was the location of the missing girls. His suspicions that Lacroix was involved in the abductions connected to the house. It was isolated. Out of sight and the man was protecting it as if he had something to hide. While that was going on inside his head, his eyes were following the movements of the two armed guards as they patrolled the grounds.

The first thing he decided definitely was the men were no professionals. They were simply men with guns, moving back and forth without any kind of measured pattern. And from their appearance they were from the same mold as Rene and Lupe. Guns for hire. Men working for money. Which usually meant the only loyalty was towards the money they earned. Lacroix might have had their attention as long as he paid them well. He would not have their hearts. There were never any absolutes when it came to owning a man's soul. Hired guns were in it for the money, not reserving a place in Heaven.

He slid the heavy Colt from its holster and checked it, making sure he was carrying a full load. Brand knew a situation could change quickly and he had no intention of being caught napping. He thought back to the way he had been taken by Rene and Lupe. There had been no question over their hostility. The intention from the moment they had *persuaded* Brand to go with them had been his imminent death. Nothing had been surer. He was going to keep that in mind once he made any move.

Brand decided his next move . . . He considered the possibility there might be others inside the house. It was something he would have to deal with if the situation arose. But come hell or high water he needed a look inside.

He spent more time watching the two guards. They both wore waterproofs over their clothes. One, short and heavy built, moved across the front of the house and headed in Brand's direction. There was no deliberation in his approach. He carried a Winchester rifle cradled across his front. He wore gaudy striped pants, knee-high tan boots. A soft-brimmed felt hat, sodden from the rain, was pulled over his shaggy dark hair. He scratched at his unshaven jaw as he walked, casually staring about him with the detached air of someone less than enthusiastic with his work.

On the other edge of the area Brand saw the second man vanish from sight down the side of the house. He figured he wasn't about to get a better opportunity. Brand reversed his Colt, holding it by the barrel as he slowly rose to his full height, still hidden by the wide trunk of the tree. He let the guard walk by, then slipped clear and stepped up behind the man. He reached out with his left hand and as with the earlier guard he knocked the felt hat clear before he slammed the butt of the Colt down across the guard's skull. The man gave a soft grunt, his knees bending as he went down. Moving quickly Brand removed the man's pistol and knife and threw them into the undergrowth. He kept the rifle close by. Brand loosened the man's belt and bound his wrists behind his back. He used the bandanna to gag the man, then dragged him deep into the bushes, not forgetting to pick up the man's hat and conceal it.

Armed with the rifle Brand crossed the open frontage until he was able to press himself against the front wall. He kept in mind the other guard, even though he couldn't be sure where the man might eventually show. Moving quickly Brand reached the main doors. When he pushed against them they opened silently and he eased himself inside.

He found himself standing in the entrance hall, with a wide stairway leading to the upper floor. The floor beneath his feet was smooth marble, the walls on either side painted plaster. A pair of chandeliers hung from the ceiling. Doors led off on either side of the hall.

He shrugged out of the heavy topcoat he was wearing to leave his arms free.

Brand became aware of the silence. It was unnaturally quiet.

Yet there was a soft, pervading smell that tainted the air. It seemed to creep out from the very walls, reaching out to envelop him. He breathed it in and felt the invasive sensation as it filled his lungs. He felt the heat now, like a thick blanket wrapping itself around him. He saw, or imagined he saw, pale wreaths of smoke — maybe mist — that floated in his direction. With a life of its own. It advanced, coiling and stretching with the sinuous grace a snake might employ.

And then he saw the man — at least he imagined it was a man — moving out from behind the staircase, gliding on silent feet as it approached him.

Tall. Lean and skeletal, the face like a grinning skull. Black hair that fell in long braids around hollow cheeks. Clad in a dark, enveloping garment that swirled around him, the exposed arms like brown twigs. Hands with long, boney fingers that flexed and curled as they pointed at Brand, The figure almost floated as it confronted him, mouth opening to expose long, near-pointed teeth.

'*Now you come to my place and now you stay . . .*'

The voice was soft, with a rolling cadence that seemed to flow from the mouth.

Brand felt his hand tighten around the rifle. It was a simple reaction to something that engendered a cold chill. This was something unexpected. Away from normality and though his mind was telling him it was some kind of trick, he still felt unnerved.

'*You want to know . . . too much . . . now you will learn what you should have left alone . . . '*

A sense of personal danger rose. Brand knew there was a threat in the words. Whatever was going on here in Lacroix's house was beyond normal and he needed to handle it. He raised his rifle, aiming at the figure. Found it so heavy in his hands.

He felt difficulty in breathing and realized he was weakening.

Damn.

It was the drifting tendrils of smoke. Despite his determination he had breathed in some of it and he could feel its effect. The soft insistence as it touched his very being. Made his thoughts waver. Pulled heavily at his eyelids. He tried to pull back but his movements were becoming sluggish. As if he was wading through molasses. Feet were getting heavier. Reactions slow . . . this was wrong . . . the rifle slipped from his grasp . . . seemed to fall to the floor in a slow curve . . . Brand dropped his right hand to the holstered Colt, fingers suddenly feeling thick and stiff

. . . and then he was on his knees . . .

The dark figure stood over him, hollow laughter coming from the gaping mouth. Brand managed to lift his head, staring up at the face and now saw Victor Lacroix returning his gaze.

'Welcome to my home, Mr. Brand. You came uninvited so whatever happens now you have brought upon yourself . . . '

The urge to drive his fist into the grinning face rose but Brand knew he would be unable to do anything. His whole body had become sluggish, a dead weight and he knew he was going to fall to the floor. When he dropped he didn't even feel when struck . . . darkness swirled around him, deep and all-consuming . . . he fell into it and just kept falling . . .

★　★　★

. . . the cell — he called it that because it couldn't have been anything else — was cold and damp. The stone walls oozed moisture. There was a small opening high up, with an iron grille over it. Brand was sprawled on the flagged floor and he could feel the chill through his clothing and a shiver ran through him. The temperature was low enough he could see his breath when he exhaled.

So much for the careful approach, he thought. *Made a damn fool mess of that.*

And what the hell had been that with the strange figure and the mist? Some kind of hallucination from — opium maybe? Some drug that had confused him? He shook the thoughts away because what he was experiencing now was no hallucination. This was real.

On the far side of his cell was a timbered door, strengthened with iron straps. He wasn't going to be shouldering that open. There was an opening set in the door, again with a barred grille in place. It was the only source of light, allowing some illumination to enter the cell. When he took a look around he realized the cell was totally bare. Devoid of any fittings.

Brand climbed to his feet, the slightest movement sending pain through his skull. The effects of whatever he had been breathing before still lingered. He realized he had been disarmed. His Colt was gone and his gunbelt. He bent over carefully and checked his right boot beneath his pants, his fingers finding the outline of the sheathed knife still in place. A small comfort. The razor-like blade might come in handy if a close up chance occurred.

It came to him that Lacroix must want something from him. *If not, why keep Brand alive?* Unbidden the disquieting thought came to him that it might simply be because Lacroix and his sister wanted Brand for their own amusement. The pair were sick enough to be playing with him. If he was right about what they had already got up to, then prolonging his life would be simply another of their damned games.

It had to be something like that.

Brand was no pawn to be used in a bargaining move. They couldn't ransom him. Even if he knew the position Brand was in McCord would not negotiate. Brand understood this and wouldn't have expected any other response from his superior. It was up to him to extract himself from Lacroix's hands. He had walked into this situation. Now it was down to him to pull himself out.

He had learned early on that Frank McCord expected his people to see their assignments all the way through without yelling for help. They were given *carte blanche* in the field. It was a known fact that McCord would back whatever they did to resolve their problems, short of mass murder. McCord had the knack of smoothing over ruffled feathers and damaged pride. He wielded power and influence and did not hesitate to use them in order to keep his department up and running. Brand had broken the rules on more than one occasion and had received the stinging rebukes McCord was capable of handing out. But as long as an assignment came to a satisfactory conclusion the verbal dressing downs were expected and accepted. His involvement with Victor Lacroix had already resulted in a degree of agitation that McCord would grumble over, but as long as the assignment resulted in its intention there was not going to be too much said and the President would be able to face the aggrieved families and offer them his sympathy over the losses they might have suffered.

One young woman already dead.

Two others still missing.

Buckman murdered in his own home and his two friends still unaccounted for.

However the affair panned out, Brand saw the body count as unacceptable. The fact the girl had been dead before he was called in did not make it any easier to accept. All it did was make Brand determined to find the missing girls and return them alive to their families

And make sure Lacroix and his sister did not walk away.

★   ★   ★

The rattle of a bolt being withdrawn brought Brand to full alert. He wasn't expecting a surprise release. Or a sudden rescue.

He stood facing the door, showing little response.

When the door swung open a heavy built, bull-necked and armed man stepped into the cell, a stubby shotgun pointing directly at Brand. Movement behind the armed man formed into Seraphina Lacroix.

Dressed in a cream silk shirt, tucked into tight black riding breeches, with gleaming high boots, she looked distinctly out of place in the gloomy cell. Her black hair was swept back from her face, sculpted into a shining coil. She paused, legs braced apart as she looked

Brand up and down.

'You look a mess, Mr. Brand.'

'Have to excuse me. I wasn't expecting visitors.'

'I fail to see the humor in your situation.'

'It's all I have left. You took away my gun so I can't shoot you. And believe me, lady, given the chance that's what I would have done.'

The beautiful face paled for a few seconds as she stared into his eyes and what she saw caught her off balance. When she recovered she forced an ugly smile on her face.

'You have caused us a great deal of upset.'

'Spoiled your blackmail scheme and your sick games.'

'I could have you killed in an instant.'

'Sure, but you haven't, so I figure you still have more of your games to play.'

'I have you where I want you, Brand. For as long as I need.'

'Do me a favor, lady. Quit the dramatics. They don't impress me.

Never did figure mumbo-jumbo had anything to get excited over.'

'Quint, perhaps Mr. Brand needs to be impressed.'

'No spells to cast? You run out of opium . . . '

'You enjoyed my introduction in the hallway? I wanted to prove my power to you. To make you aware I am not a charlatan.'

'No need because I don't give a damn about your games.'

'*Games?*' Seraphina's anger rose. Uncontrolled. 'Damn you . . . you think I am playing games?'

Brand kept his gaze on Seraphina, aware the shotgun man, Quint, was moving in, his weapon off-cock as he swung the stock in a lazy arc. Whatever else he might have been Quint was not fast. His stocky build kept his movements slow. Brand eased to the side as the shotgun came in his direction, following up with a hard shoulder that pushed Quint off balance. As the big man stumbled off-balance

Brand clubbed him across the side of his thick neck, palm-edge delivered with considerable force; it was one of Kito's strikes Brand had been forced to practice many times over, with the martial arts master drilling into his pupil the need to hit hard and fast, unmindful of the damage the blow could inflict. Quint gave a hoarse grunt, falling sideways as his nervous system reacted to the blow. As he dropped to his knees Brand snatched the shotgun from his unresisting grip.

A shrill yell came from Seraphina. Out the corner of his eye, Brand saw her right hand reaching behind her. A small silver revolver was clutched in her hand when it reappeared, the muzzle centering on Brand.

He wrenched his body around, shotgun following, aware Seraphina had the advantage. The revolver flashed a sparkle of flame, the sound of the shot hard in the confines of the cell.

Brand felt the slug bite as it hit, but he had already made his own strike.

The wood butt of the shotgun made a solid sound as it cracked across the side of Seraphina's face. Her head was snapped to one side. She uttered a surprised cry as the force of the blow sent her stumbling, losing her balance and stretching full length across the floor of the cell.

Reversing the shotgun Brand eased back the hammers. He glanced down at Quint. The man lay still. Unconscious. Brand bent over him and searched his pockets. Found four more shells for the shotgun. The man had no other weapon on him.

Standing over Seraphina he picked up the revolver she had dropped. Checked the loads. Six in the cylinder. One fired. Small caliber, .32, thankfully he accepted. He could feel the burn from the shot she had put into him now. The slug had buried itself in the tight muscle of his left shoulder. It was painful and it was going to slow him, but Brand figured it wouldn't stop him doing what he had to do. He tucked the revolver behind his belt.

Something made him look closer at Seraphina. He checked for a pulse. There wasn't one.

'Magic isn't working now,' he said quietly. 'So much for the Creole Curse.'

When he stepped out of the cell he closed the door and slid the bolt home, pausing to check the stone passage that extended either side of the cell. The right hand one showed footprints on the damp surface. One set was small. Like a woman's . . . Seraphina. It was as good an indication as he was likely to get. Brand followed the passage and took the left turn at the end.

Soft sounds reached him and he paused. The way ahead was shadowed despite the lamps fixed to the walls. Yet there was enough illumination to show him the barred doors spaced along the walls.

In the first cell he found the two missing girls. When he showed himself they drew back on the low cots, faces pale and drawn. Their clothes were soiled and torn. Faces bruised and dirty. Neither of them said a word.

'I'll get you out of there soon as I can. Give me a little time to . . . '

A scuff of boot leather alerted him. Brand turned from the cell, the shotgun lifting. One of the pair who stepped into view recognized Brand and gave a yell, his hand snaking for the gun tucked behind his belt.

There was no time for hesitation. Brand centered the raised shotgun and fired off both barrels. In the narrow passage the effect was devastating. The double-charge caught both men chest high, shredding bodies and clothing, flinging them back in a welter of bloodied flesh and clothing. The twin shots echoed loudly within the confines of the stone walls. One of the girls began to scream.

Brand opened the shotgun and shucked out the smoking shells, replacing them with fresh loads. The act of firing off the shotgun sent pain through his shoulder and he leaned against the wall until the worst passed. He could feel the wet blood soaking through his shirt.

It would be nice, he thought, *if I could come through an assignment without getting shot, or stabbed, or beaten.* Somehow he couldn't see that happening. He decided it had something to do with the kind of people he was always forced to deal with.

He turned back towards the cells, moving by the two girls and checked the other barred doors. He passed a couple before he located an occupied one. Two men. In a similar condition to the girls. Unshaven, clothing stained and bloody. It appeared he had found Coleman and Dalton. When he called their names they raised their heads and stared at him. It took a few seconds before one of them responded.

'The shooting . . . was that you?'

Brand nodded.

'Can you get us out . . . please.'

'That's the idea. I just need to find keys to open these cells.'

'They have one of our friends as well. Cyrus Buckman.'

The man dragged himself off the cot and moved to the barred door, fingers gripping the metal.

'You have to find him too . . . '

'Buckman escaped. Reached home but he was followed and killed.'

'*Cyrus dead.*' The second man drew himself up off the cot. 'You have to stop him. Lacroix. The man is a maniac. They both are. Him and that damned sister of his.'

'We'll talk about that later. First I need to get you people out of here.'

Brand saw the sudden stare of alarm in the face of the man at the door. He was staring over Brand's shoulder, mouth forming words.

The faintest whisper of sound came to him then and Brand spun around. Found himself face to face with a grinning Mulatto. The man was as tall as Brand, with big shoulders under his sleeveless shirt. He possessed a powerful chest and muscled arms. Thick black hair hung in oily braids to his shoulders. His lips were peeled back from his teeth, eyes wide and glassy.

When he moved it was with effortless speed, his large hands grasping the shotgun. He wrenched it from Brand's grip and threw it aside, then caught hold of Brand by his shirt front and shook him like a child with a doll. When he let go Brand was hurled across the passage, crashing against the opposite wall. The impact stunned him for a few seconds and he saw the big man coming at him, still with a pleased smile on his broad, dark face.

This feller likes to play with his food.

Big and heavy as he was the Mulatto moved fast and he was on Brand swiftly, those big hands ready to do damage. Brand reached behind him for Seraphina's revolver. It was not there. It must have slipped from his belt during the struggle.

The Mulatto took hold of Brand's shirt again, swinging him back and forth and the expression on his face said he was enjoying himself. One hand formed into a fist and he pounded at the bullet wound in Brand's shoulder. A grunt of pain escaped Brand's lips.

He drew back his right arm, fist bunched and he struck hard at the other man's nose. He felt the nose crunch. Blood streamed from the nostrils, bright and heavy. The Mulatto grunted. Shook his head, spraying blood. Brand knew it had hurt. The nose was sensitive to pain and in truth was a weak part of the body. Brand struck again — a third time. The man's nose collapsed. Blood was gushing heavily and tears formed in his eyes. As strong as he was the pain, extreme now, had an effect and the Mulatto let go of Brand, flinging him aside, and clamped his hands over his ruined nose, blood pulsing between his fingers. Brand slumped against the stone wall. He grabbed at the wall lamp hanging close and swung it hard. The metal frame slammed against the Mulatto's skull, tearing a gash that began to bleed.

Brand struck out again but the man swung up a powerful arm and knocked the lamp out of Brand's grip. Blood streamed down the side of the Mulatto's face. None of his injuries seemed to be slowing the man down. He lunged forward, hands extended, fingers sliding around Brand's neck. Brand knew if the man gained his hold he would have a lesser chance of breaking free. He dropped his chin to his chest and rammed his right shoulder into the Mulatto's chest, encircled the solid body and lifted his adversary off his feet. It took a lot of effort. The Mulatto was a heavy man. It was what Brand was hoping would give him the advantage. The moment the man's feet left the ground Brand swiveled, let himself fall and took them both down, maneuvering himself so he was on top as they crashed to the stone floor of the passage. The moment they landed Brand freed his arms from around the man's body, snatched handfuls of hair and smashed the Mulatto's head down hard against the passage floor. The thud of the contact was audible. The Mulatto's eyes opened wide with shock. Brand gave him no chance to recover. He repeatedly raised and slammed the man's head onto the stone. It was only when worms of blood, seeping out from under the broken skull, showed did he stop. Brand slipped sideways, sweat beading his face. He let his breathing calm before he moved.

As he slowly climbed to his feet he saw the ring of keys hooked over the Mulatto's belt. He freed the ring and crossed to the cells, picking up the dropped revolver and shotgun. He found he could barely use his left arm. Blood had spread across his shirt from the wound. He tucked the shotgun under his arm and fumbled with the keys until he was able to unlock the cell holding the two men. They stumbled out of the cell.

'Take this,' Brand said, holding out the shotgun. 'It's loaded so don't point it my way.'

Jerome Coleman took the weapon.

'Not as classy as my Foxworth, but it will do.'

When Brand opened the girls' cell they simply stood staring at him. Brand could understand their hesitation. In their position he would have been just as suspicious. It was Henry Dalton who stepped by and into the cell, speaking gently to the frightened young women.

'They killed Netta Delacort didn't they?' Coleman said in a hushed voice.

Brand nodded.

'They are both mad,' Coleman said. 'Sick in the head. They do things. Terrible things because they enjoy hurting people. I still find it hard to understand why they would . . . '

'You just said it. They are *sick*.'

'The woman is the worst . . . I . . . I can't describe what she made us do. I only know I'm ashamed I allowed myself to be drawn into their games . . . all three of us. We were fools. We let ourselves be drawn in. Drink. The gambling. Then when we came here it was worse. At first it was like a stupid game. More drink. Then the opium. We were like kids in a candy store. Took what they offered and by the time we realized it was too late . . . by God I want a chance to make that woman pay . . . '

'Too late for that. Seraphina is dead.'

'That is the best news you could have given me. What about Lacroix?'

'No sign of him.'

'He'll be in that damned place again. *The Creole Queen*. It's his second home.'

'I'll find him.'

'When we were here and under the influence of that damn drug, they did things in front of us. The pair of them. Brother and sister. Even though I was not in a sound state I knew it was wrong. The things they were doing. Naked . . . and then making those girls join in. That Mulatto you killed . . . he was one of them. Do you understand what I'm saying? Those terrible things . . . how can people do that . . . '

Henry Dalton was moving out of the cell, an arm around the shoulders of the trembling girls. Coleman fell silent, his face ashen as he recalled the things he had seen.

'I've told them we're going home,' Dalton said. 'Back to their families.'

Brand nodded. 'Stay with them. Coleman, you bring up the rear. Everyone stay close.'

When they passed the bodies of the guards Brand had put down earlier he ushered them quickly by, then crouched and searched the bloodied bodies. Found loaded revolvers he took, tucking Seraphina's small caliber pistol behind his belt. His newly acquired weapons were Colt Peacemakers. Forty-five caliber and both fully loaded. The heavy weapons felt good in his hands after Seraphina's lightweight gun. He carried one Colt, thrust the second one behind his belt. His left arm was still hanging limp at his side so he decided not to risk handling a full sized pistol in his left hand.

He caught up with the others as they walked the cold, damp passageway. They eventually reached stone steps leading upwards.

'They brought us this way,' Dalton said. 'Comes out in Lacroix's study.'

Brand led the way to the heavy wooden door. It stood ajar. He eased it wide with the muzzle of his Colt.

The big room was expensively furnished, the walls lined with books and hung paintings. A log fire burned in the big hearth. At the far end of the room, directly under the main window, was a huge oak desk. Lacroix's presumably. On the top lay Brand's holstered Colt and beside it the rifle he'd had when he entered the house. He took the opportunity to dispose of Seraphina's pistol, strapped on his belt and checked his Colt. He handed one of his acquired revolvers to Dalton. The man took it with a reluctant acknowledgment.

'*In case*,' Brand said.

He kept the other revolver in his

belt, recalling the guard he had seen outside.

'There any others in the house?' he asked.

'To be truthful we don't know,' Coleman said. 'By the time Lacroix brought us here we had already had too much to drink to notice things like that.'

'I'm ashamed to say I had other things on my mind,' Dalton said. 'Look, can we get these girls out of here quickly. Whatever happens to me is of less importance than getting these poor children home.'

Brand had spotted a drinks cabinet and crossed to it. He pushed glasses aside to get to a full bottle of Lacroix's best whiskey. He pulled the cork with his teeth and took a hefty swallow, eyes watering as the liquor coursed down his throat.

'Is that important right now?' Dalton said.

Brand indicated his blood-soaked shoulder. 'Medicinal,' he said, his voice husky from the whiskey. 'That *is* important.'

He dropped the bottle, made a final check on the rifle, then led the way to the door. The hallway was silent. Empty. Brand had a fleeting vision of the scene when he had entered earlier. The strange smoky atmosphere. The weird figure that had appeared, taunting him. That eerie, skeletal image that had morphed into Seraphina just before he blacked out . . .

The main door opened easily. It was still raining. Brand eased through and took a long look around. The area seemed deserted. He didn't believe it for a minute. Some inner sense told him they were not alone. He had no idea how much time had elapsed since he had entered the house. He had to assume long enough for Lacroix to have added to the armed guard around the place.

'We need some kind of carriage,' Coleman said quietly. 'I recall the stables are over to the left.'

'You lead the girls there,' Brand said. 'Get inside and see what you can find.'

'Where are you going?'

'Maybe I can create a diversion. Just get to the stable. I'll join you.'

★ ★ ★

Brand slipped back inside and returned to the study. He crossed to the window behind the desk and freed the latch so he could slide the windows open. He crossed to the drinks cabinet and uncorked a number of bottles of spirit. He laid a wet trail of liquor across the room, tipping more across the desk and down the side. He led the trail of liquor up to the hearth then used a fire-iron to rake out burning embers. Standing back he watched the pale flames start, following the trail of liquor across the floor as the vapor ignited. Brand retreated to the door and watched the flames expand as they took hold. The tendrils crawled up the side of the desk and spread over the top. Smoke began to show, drifting. The slight breeze coming in through the open window fanned the flames.

Brand slipped out through the front door and cut along the front of the house in the direction of the stables, where the doors were being eased open. He met Dalton.

'We found a handy carriage. Enough room for us all. Jerome is handling the horses. He's better at it than me.'

Brand followed him inside the shadowed building where Coleman had a two-horse team already in harness. He was coupling them, glancing up when Brand joined him.

'Haven't done this for a long time.'

The two girls were in the rear seat of the carriage, muffled up in thick blankets. Dalton joined them, sitting between them and speaking in a quiet voice that appeared to be keeping them settled.

Coleman drew the reins across the backs of the team and climbed up onto the front seat.

'I'll clear the doors,' Brand said. 'When you get outside drive down to the road and head for the city. Do not stop for anything. Get them to Doctor Regis Marcellus. Understand?'

Coleman nodded. 'What about you?'

'There are things to do here. Hopefully my little diversion will keep Lacroix's men busy.'

'*Oh?* What did you do, set his house on fire . . . ' Brand's silent expression dawned and Coleman managed a faint smile. 'I must remember not to get on your bad side, Mister . . . ?'

'Brand. Now get the hell out of here and keep those horses moving. Don't wait for me. I have my own horse nearby.'

Brand pushed the stable doors wide.

Coleman flicked the team into motion and as the carriage rolled clear, out of the corner of his eye he saw wreaths of smoke issuing from one of the ground floor windows of the house. The image slid behind him as he cracked the whip over the team, urging them into a fast trot in the direction of the road. He barely held the team back as it took the turn off the drive and onto the road that would lead back to New Orleans.

He picked up a sound of raised voices . . . and then the crackle of gunfire . . .

★   ★   ★

. . . smoke was thickening as it left the window. It seemed Brand's diversionary tactic was working better than he had anticipated. It also brought a number of armed figures into view as they emerged from behind the house and the thick foliage. He counted four of them. One was the guard he had spotted earlier. They gathered in a tight group, staring at the smoke billowing from the window, indecision stopping them until one caught sight of Brand framed in the stable doors.

He yelled a warning to his partners and they followed his lead, bringing their guns to bear on Brand. The crackle of rapid fire sent slugs in Brand's direction. The distance made it difficult for accurate shooting without a steady aim. Brand heard the thud of slugs hitting the stable doors as he dropped to a crouch, sending wood splinters flying. He shouldered the rifle, aware his weak left arm was not going to support the heavy weapon for long, and sucked in a steadying breath as he aimed, held his targets and loosed off a number of shots. He saw one man fall back. A second stumbled, clutching at his shooting arm. With the weight of his rifle aggravating his own arm Brand let the rifle drop to the ground and cleared his Colt from the holster, the hammer going back as he extended his shooting arm, ignoring the gunfire directed at him. He briefly recalled the advice from Whitehead, the armorer at McCord's headquarters.

'*Fast draw doesn't mean a thing if you can't hit your target. Take that extra second to center your shot before you fire.'*

He fired, altered his aim and held again. Felt something tug at his shirt and forced himself to cock and fire again. He placed a slug in one man chest high. Saw him fall back a step before he dropped. The remaining shooter made to turn aside to narrow his bulk, then gave a sudden jerk as a .45 slug slammed into the side of his skull and shut him down before he fell to the ground. Movement drew Brand's attention. It was the man with the bullet wound in his arm, changing his revolver to his left hand. Brand didn't hesitate. He turned his Colt in the man's direction. Saw the alarm on the man's face in the scant second before Brand hit him with a pair of close-fired shots that drove him groundwards in an instant.

He crossed to the men he had put down. One was still alive. Spilling blood but conscious. He glared at Brand.

'You get it done?' he said.

Brand nodded. 'You took your last payday for this outfit.'

The man grimaced. 'Just tell me one thing. Is that bitch dead?'

'Seraphina? She cast her last spell.'

'Almost worth getting shot to hear that.'

'Not your favorite lady?'

'Evil through and through that one. Hadn't been for the good money. Hell, you know.'

'I don't see Lacroix around.'

The man spat blood from his mouth.

'He left a while before you showed up. If he ain't here he's back in town at that fancy palace.'

'That's what I was guessing,' Brand said.

He heard the man groan. His body stretched out as he let go his last breath.

Brand could hear the subdued crackle of the fire as it gained a hold inside the house. Glass cracked from the heat in another window. He turned and went back inside the stables.

Minutes later he was herding the rest of the horses into the open where they scattered. With that done he retrieved his rifle and walked away, heading to where he had left his own horse tied up. He took his time. His shoulder was still giving him pain and it had bled some more. Doc Marcellus was going to have one more patient to deal with when Brand got back to New Orleans.

* * *

It was close on dark when Brand reached *The Creole Queen*. With the Mardi Gras virtually over the streets were quieter. The crowds had diminished, leaving behind the litter that was associated with the mass celebrations. Before he reached *The Creole Queen* Brand saw the place was in semi-shadow. The main doors were closed. Which in itself was unusual. He dismounted and tied his horse to one of the single metal hitching posts edging the boardwalk. His disheveled appearance and the blood staining his left shoulder drew a number of curious stares from the few people braving the still falling rain as he made his way to the alley running alongside the building. Brand ignored the interest. When he reached the gates that blocked off the delivery yard behind the saloon Brand pulled both of his Colts, gave them a cursory check before he paused. The last time he had entered the area he had been confronted by Julienne Dubois and his henchmen. Since that episode Brand had learned a great deal more about Lacroix's hired help. Their determined stance to back any play by their employer had provided him with the knowledge he was dealing with a relentless bunch who had little respect for anyone who happened to stand against them or their paymaster.

That knowledge gave Brand an edge. He could play that game with a clear conscience. There was a need to even the score and Brand was able to put himself in the frame of mind to do just that with good reason.

Netta Delacort was dead. Cyrus Buckman was dead. So was Lyle Kelso, the young police officer Noonan had assigned to the case. Brand didn't even consider the dead from Lacroix's side. Not even Seraphina. He didn't give a god damn about them. For a fleeting moment he thought about the Creole Curse. Voodoo and the long held belief that the dead could be brought back to life as Zombies. If that happened to Lacroix's crew there would be a substantial number of them walking around. He shrugged off the notion with a mirthless smile on his lips. That would be the last thing he needed. He was still having enough trouble with the living.

He pushed against the gates and felt them give. As soon as there was enough room to let him through Brand stepped into the open yard.

Remember your enemies are only human as well. No man wants to die early if he can avoid it. If they face a man who shows his strength it will make them pause. Use that hesitation to your advantage.

Another of Kito's observations. In truth it held because most men would take that second longer before they opened fire. Brand didn't have that restriction. Once he knew a man was intent on doing him harm his survival instinct took over and he responded without any kind of hesitation.

Both handguns were cocked as he broached the yard, eyes searching, his body alert for any kind of opposition.

He recalled the layout from last time. The livery stable. There were no wheeled buggies present this time. He concentrated on the wooden loading platform and the door that led inside the building.

And a dark-skinned, armed figure moving onto the loading platform. The rifle in the man's hands already being raised in Brand's direction.

No hesitation . . .

Brand's right hand Colt lifted, armed extended. He held, then triggered his shot. Saw the rifleman fall back against the door frame as the big .45 slug thudded into his chest. He was pinned to the frame for a couple of seconds before his legs gave beneath him and he dropped.

Moving forward Brand made for the loading platform. Spotted a second would-be shooter emerging from the doorway. He brought both revolvers into play triggering shots from each weapon. As the solid sound of the shots faded and the man went down, he saw a third man slip into view from the doorway. Brand opened fire without missing a step and the man fell across the loading platform, the rifle he was carrying slipping from his grip.

Increasing his pace, Brand went up the steps and made for the door. He fired a couple of distraction shots through the opening, then ducked inside, moving quickly to the left and pressed his back to the wall.

He was in a storage area that had a door at the far side that would likely lead into *The Creole Queen* proper. Boxes and barrels displayed the casino's liquor. Other cartons held foodstuffs. Everything was neatly displayed and Brand took a guess that the orderliness would be down to Julienne Dubois. He could imagine the Frenchman being well organized.

Brand dropped to reduce his bulk behind a stack of wooden casks. Saw muzzle flash, followed by the crack of a handgun. He heard the slug pound the wall overhead.

Then a chuckle of laughter.

'Very commendable, *Monsieur* Brand. I doubt you will be able to avoid every shot. I suggested last time you were here that this part of *The Creole Queen* was not for you. You have chosen to ignore my warning. *Ainsi soit-il*.'

Brand heard a soft scuffle of sound. Saw a dark figure moving across the storehouse. Too heavy-footed to be Dubois so he decided the Frenchman was not alone. Which he had expected. It caused him to wonder just how many extra guns Dubois had with him. While he debated his next move Brand swapped the empty casings for fresh loads from his belt loops, reloading both pistols. He could feel fresh blood oozing from his shoulder as his rapid movements disturbed the wound,

To his left there was more movement. A pair of figures now, crowding each other as they made their move, and that brief clumsiness allowed Brand his moment.

He rose from his cover, threw a quick shot in Dubois's direction, then swiveled and faced the hesitant pair as they broke cover. The pair of Colts crackled with sound as Brand opened up with a steady burst of fire, his shots delivered with accuracy as he set himself and picked his targets. One man went down in a flurry of arms and legs, slamming face down on the hardwood floor. His erstwhile companion, cursing loudly, triggered his own gun with what Brand regarded as total recklessness. The slugs were wide of the mark. Brand thrust out his right arm, saw the look on the other's face as he touched the trigger and put a .45 slug between the eyes. The man went over without a sound and stretched out alongside his already dead partner.

The moment he put the second man down Brand turned and strode across the open floor, both guns up and cocked as he saw Dubois move from his own cover, still confident as he acknowledged Brand's ability.

'Make this your play,' Brand said, 'and you get what they did. I want Lacroix and if I have to I'll go through you, Dubois.'

'Each man chooses his own destiny. Mine at this moment is to stand between you and *your* choice.'

'Hell,' Brand said, 'the last thing I need is any of your damned French quotations.'

Dubois let a thin smile curl his lips as he took in Brand's words, but he was left behind when Brand's guns swept into line and he put a number of .45 slugs in the Frenchman's body before he even realized he was way too slow to match the American's move. Brand walked on by the slumped body and kicked open the door Dubois had been covering.

★　★　★

The gunfire from the rear of the building alerted Lacroix. It came as no surprise to him. If he had admitted the truth he had been expecting it. He had experienced a feeling that warned him. He knew something was wrong. That events had conspired against him. Anticipation of a powerful challenge gripped him. A challenge that threatened his very life. He had closed *The Creole Queen* early, making sure the place was empty before securing the front doors and retreating to the gaming room, with Dubois and his men spread throughout the building.

It had been a long time since Lacroix felt insecure. Closeted in the room, surrounded by his possessions and though knowing armed men were looking out for him, the man understood fear. At this moment his wealth, the association with men of influence and power, none of it offered him any comfort. He could not understand why. He was Victor Lacroix. A powerful man with the strength of his beliefs in the darker world to bolster his confidence. With Seraphina at his side he wielded the mysterious influence of the voodoo craft. Together they drew in those weaker than themselves and used that weakness to gain control, while enjoying the salacious and forbidden desires that bound them together as more than brother and sister. It was something they had practiced for years and coupled with Seraphina's almost unquenchable lust they had practiced the art, using it to ensnare others. Giving their jaded senses the needs they had held in check in frustration for so

216

long. Once ensnared it allowed Lacroix and Seraphina to manipulate their compliant victims into positions where they would willingly pay whatever was asked in order to keep their guilty secrets from being revealed.

The young women they abducted were used to draw in the gullible. A miscalculation by Lacroix had come about when he had traded up from those who would be less likely to be missed by taking a higher class of girls for his clients. It had seemed to be working until Netta Delacort had defied Lacroix and his sister, and in a moment of rage Seraphina had attacked and killed her.

The death of the young woman had been the catalyst that had brought about the rebellion of Jerome Coleman and Henry Dalton. Until he could decide how to handle the situation Lacroix had imprisoned them, along with Cyrus Buckman. Seraphina — convinced she could deal with the problem — had attempted to drug and seduce Buckman in order to silence his concerns. Her plan misfired when Buckman defied her and broke out of the cellars under the house.

Lacroix had sent his paid assassin — Doctor Vallejo — to silence Buckman. Although he did succeed, Vallejo was confronted by the man named Brand and killed himself.

Too much had conspired against Lacroix from the moment the man from the Justice Department showed up in New Orleans. He had resisted every attempt to silence him and Lacroix found himself losing men and credibility. In a moment of reflection he admitted that Brand was outsmarting him. The man seemed to possess a charmed life that enabled him to walk through fire and fury. For once in his life Victor Lacroix felt powerless. He was being backed into a corner and he did not enjoy the feeling.

Something had warned him matters were moving towards an end. He had closed *The Creole Queen*, closeting himself in the building while he took time to consider his next move.

He sat himself in the room off the main salon, at one of the gaming tables, forcing himself to go through the motions of a turn of solitaire. A distraction while he considered the matters at hand. This was the private space where privileged clients were brought to gamble and drink. Where Lacroix's special girls were on hand to provide sexual stimulation. While it brought in money it allowed Lacroix to study each patron and decide who would be his next *victim*. Those with the best wealth and influence were the ones chosen. They were feted, indulged, and once chosen would be invited to Lacroix's home outside the city where they would be able to take the next step into depravity, unaware they were being deliberately selected.

The scheme had been extremely successful. Already a number of New Orleans's elite were on the hook. Paying the price for their indulgences. It had seemed Lacroix might be able to play his games without pause. Until Seraphina's wantonness had pushed her to excess and the death of Netta Delacort.

Victor Lacroix loved his sister — physically as well as with familial loyalty — and he was left with no choice but to attempt to cover up her reckless act that left them with a dead young woman and too many witnesses. It seemed everything was conspiring to drag them down and Lacroix was plagued with uncertainties . . .

Those concerns manifested themselves into the sound of gunfire coming from the storage area behind the room he was seated in. When the gunfire came closer Lacroix started with a jerk, raising himself from the stupor he had developed. His hand jerked and he spilled expensive whiskey across the green baize tabletop.

He called out to his two remaining gunmen in the room with him. They kicked up from their chairs, hands snaking for the holstered revolvers they carried.

'Deal with it,' Lacroix said. 'If it's that bastard, Brand, I want him dead this time.'

The bought gunmen, who earned well being on his payroll, moved across the room.

They had barely taken more than a few steps when the door to the rear area was kicked open with enough force to smash it back against the wall, one set of hinges breaking free.

A moving figure was briefly framed in the opening, holding a weapon in each hand . . . and despite their expectations, the pair of gunmen were left standing as the pair of .45 Colts spat flame and smoke, filling the room with their thunder . . . the closest of the pair was dropped to the floor with slugs hammering his chest . . . his partner seemingly given more time, managed to loose off a single shot before he was hit himself. One slug in the body, a second that cored in above his left eye and sheared off the back of his skull in a shower of bloody gore.

Lacroix made a clumsy grab for the pistol he wore under his expensive coat, fingers clawing at the butt. The shot from Brand's Colt went through his coat, mangling his gun hand and went through to dig into his chest. In sudden pain Lacroix pulled his hand free from beneath his coat and stared in horror at the bloody wound where the slug had taken off fingers and left behind dripping stumps. He sank back in the seat, moaning in pain and sheer fright.

Brand stood a few feet away, a pistol in each hand. He was in a disheveled condition. His clothing was marked and there was a bloody stain, leaking fresh blood, in his left shoulder. But it was the bleak, taut expression on his face that held Lacroix's gaze. His eyes were fixed on Lacroix. Unblinking and without a trace of compassion.

'Too many,' he said, 'dead and suffering because of you and that damn sister of yours.'

'It was only . . . '

Brand put a second slug into Lacroix's other shoulder, the slug tearing a bloody hole as it exited. Lacroix screamed, slumping back.

'You think Netta Delacort felt scared? When she realized she was going to die. What do you think Mr. Lacroix? *What do you think?*'

'It was a mistake she died. Seraphina didn't mean to kill her . . . '

'Well she's paid for that mistake. Seraphina is dead too. That's how I left her before I burned down that house of yours.'

'*Dead? Seraphina? No . . . *'

The words came out in a scream of despair as Lacroix pushed himself up off his seat, making a futile lunge across the table.

Brand steadied his hands, the muzzles of his pistols on Lacroix as he fired and fired again. Not stopping until the hammers dropped on empty chambers and smoke curled from the hot muzzles.

Victor Lacroix thudded to the floor,

his body riddled and bloody from multiple wounds. As Brand calmly reloaded he watched the man go through his death throes, his blood seeping from the wounds until his heart stopped beating and he lay still.

On the table lay the cards Lacroix had been using. Speckles of blood had splashed onto the table and the cards.

'Now that's a dead man's hand if I ever saw one,' Brand said to himself.

* * *

It took almost a week to bring matters to a close. Documents found in the safe in Lacroix's office in the casino revealed a long list of names who had been blackmailed by the man and his sister. In the files were incriminating photos implicating members of New Orleans high society caught in revealing positions. There was also documentary evidence of financial arrangements for the money being paid to Lacroix to keep secrets under wraps. Inspector

Don Noonan, once he saw this evidence, had everything destroyed, overseeing it himself, keeping names and faces out of the public eye. A number of the victims of Lacroix's blackmail turned out to be members of the city police department. Without pointing the finger as such, Brand made certain that it was known that a number of his superiors were on the list. Suddenly all criticism over Inspector Noonan's performance was gone. Those who knew their names had been identified fell silent.

Noonan could have made things difficult for the men above him, but he stayed silent. They knew who they were and that was enough for him.

The rescued girls, returned to their families, would have to make their own peace with what had happened. It would take time, but they at least were still alive. The family of Netta Delacort, after burying their daughter, would have their own healing to face. As would Lyle Kelso's family who had lost their son in the course of his duty. Noonan made it *his* duty to ensure Kelso would receive the police department's highest commendation.

When Lacroix's crimes were made known across the city the people who had claimed to be his friends suddenly and collectively drew back, not wanting to find themselves in any way associated with the unsavory things he had been involved in. *Human nature,* Brand decided, *always chose the less troublesome trail.*

After Doc Marcellus extracted the small lead pellet from his shoulder and dealt with the other scrapes and bruises, Brand sent a telegram to McCord, detailing the events leading to the conclusion of the assignment. He received a reply two days later. McCord, with his usual brevity, told Brand the President had been informed and passed on his thanks. There was even a perfunctory acknowledgment from McCord himself, with the rider that at least Brand hadn't managed to burn New Orleans to the ground, albeit one house, and a question as to when Brand would be returning to Washington as there was another piece of business waiting for his attention.

'He sounds like a man with work on his mind,' Noonan commented when Brand showed him McCord's message.

'Not one to let the grass grow under his feet.'

Noonan managed a smile as he surveyed both his and Brand's shoulder slings.

'Damned if we both don't look a pair.'

He put out his free hand and took Brand's. 'Come back some time. This can be a hell of a nice town when it gets the chance.'

'But never *too* peaceful I hope.'

'Wouldn't want to disappoint you, Mr. Brand.'

That, thought Brand as he walked out of the office and made his way to the street, was less likely to happen than him ending up anywhere with peace and goodwill surrounding him. As long as he worked for McCord he was going to find himself up against the kind of situations that had become his stock in trade — and to be honest he wouldn't have it any other way . . .

We do hope that you have enjoyed reading this large print book.

Did you know that all of our titles are available for purchase?

We publish a wide range of high quality large print books including:
Romances, Mysteries, Classics
General Fiction
Non Fiction and Westerns

Special interest titles available in large print are:
The Little Oxford Dictionary
Music Book, Song Book
Hymn Book, Service Book

Also available from us courtesy of Oxford University Press:
Young Readers' Dictionary
(large print edition)
Young Readers' Thesaurus
(large print edition)

For further information or a free brochure, please contact us at:
Ulverscroft Large Print Books Ltd.,
The Green, Bradgate Road, Anstey,
Leicester, LE7 7FU, England.
Tel: (00 44) **0116 236 4325**
Fax: (00 44) **0116 234 0205**

BANDIT'S GOLD

Alex Frew

When Joe Flint meets Matt Harper and Pete Brogan, he is enticed by their tales of gold and mystery. They tell of a legendary Mexican leader who funded his reign during the Civil War through a criminal network. Drawn in by the promise of fortune, he follows his new friends. But along the way, they are attacked. Flint learns too late that he has put himself in the hands of madmen. Will he find his fortune? Will he even get out alive?

THE SMILING HANGMAN

Owen G. Irons

The town of King's Creek is in uproar. Young Matthew Lydell has been found guilty of murdering Janet Teasdale, daughter of a local banker. Lydell is to be hanged. But the town marshal has been delaying proceedings, and sent for a hangman from the county seat. The hangman arrives quietly, unnoticed. He tours the jail and the town, smiling, always smiling. What secret lies behind that smile, and what intentions does he have for the Colt riding on his hip . . . ?

FUGITIVE LAWMAN

Jethro Kyle

Down on his luck in Chicago, Dale Carnak ends up applying for work with the Pinkerton National Detective Agency. Spotted by an old acquaintance, he is swiftly hired, and agrees to the risky assignment of infiltrating the Fraser Gang — even participating in a train robbery. But a series of misunderstandings sees Carnak become a fugitive, on the run with the rest of the outlaws. Then the bandits begin to suspect that their newest recruit is not who he claims to be . . .